ALEXANDER THE GREAT ROCKS THE WORLD

BY VICKY ALVEAR SHECTER Ω ILLUSTRATED BY TERRY NAUGHTON

DARBY CREEK PUBLISHING

To Michael, who's shown me how to lighten up, both in life and in my writing.

To Matthew and Aliya, who inspired me—
and continue to inspire me—with their questions and creativity.

And finally, to Bruce, who believed in me all along.

Cataloging-in-Publication

Shecter, Vicky.
Alexander the Great rocks the world / by Vicky Alvear Shecter.
        p. ; cm.
    ISBN-13: 978-1-58196-045-7
    ISBN-10: 1-58196-045-X
    Summary: Sixteen-year-old Alexander was left in charge of Macedon when his father, the king, went on a business trip. When a barbarian tribe attacked Macedon, Alexander led the army against them, and won! By 18, Alexander was named a general of the army; at 20 he ruled all of Ancient Greece; at 25 he had conquered most of ancient Persia. By 32, he was really King of the World!
    1. Alexander, the Great, 356–323 B.C.—Juvenile literature. 2. Generals—Greece—Biography—Juvenile literature. 3. Greece—Kings and rulers—Biography—Juvenile literature. 4. Greece—History—Macedonian Expansion, 359–323 B.C.—Juvenile literature. [1. Alexander, the Great, 356–323 B.C. 2. Generals—Greece—Biography. 3. Greece—Kings and rulers—Biography. 4. Greece—History—Macedonian Expansion, 359–323 B.C.] I. Title. II. Author.
    DF234.2 .S54 2006
    938/.07/092 B dc22
    OCLC: 63178503

Text copyright © 2006 by Vicky Alvear Shecter
Cover art by Terry Naughton
Design by Kelly Rabideau
Copyright © 2006 Darby Creek Publishing

Published by **Darby Creek Publishing**
7858 Industrial Parkway
Plain City, OH 43064
www.darbycreekpublishing.com

Printed in Italy

1 2 3 4 5 6 7 8 9

PHOTO CREDITS

15: phalanx/used with permission by Dr. Gary Gutchess and Dr. Paul Cartledge. **24:** discus thrower, runners, wrestlers/used with permission by Hellenic-art.com. **25:** torch relay/used with permission by Hellenic-art.com. **33:** Aristotle bust © Phil Sigin/istockphoto.com. **42:** kopis/used with permission by Hellenic-art.com; Athena © Andreas Guskos/Dreamstime.com. **43:** greaves/used with permission by Hellenic-art.com; Shield of Achilles/reproduced with kind permission of Reading University Library; Spartan shield © Paul Moore/Bigstockfoto.com. **44:** Alexander bust/used with permission by Hellenic-art.com. **45:** Alexander and Bucephalas/used with permission by Hellenic-art.com. **46:** lion statue © Jona Lendering. **47:** Alexander statue © Andrew Michael Chugg. **59:** Alexander addresses officers © Andrew Michael Chugg. **61:** Alexander and physician © Andrew Michael Chugg. **62:** Greek woman/J. Mohr Smith/used with permission by Dr. Tara Maginnis. **66:** Luxor relief /used with permission by Jona Lendering and Maria Van Houte. **68:** laying out Alexandria © Andrew Michael Chugg. **71:** scythe chariots © Andrew Michael Chugg. **75:** common coins/used with permission by cngcoins.com; Persian women © Andrew Michael Chugg. **78:** proskynesis © Jona Lendering. **79:** tunic/Leon A. Heuzy/used with permission by Dr. Tara Maginnis; trousers/Auguste Racinet/used with permission by Dr. Tara Maginnis; Persian costume/Braun and Schneider/used with permission by C. Otis Sweezey. **82:** Alexander and Roxane © Andrew Michael Chugg. **83:** Alexander mourns Cleitus © Andrew Michael Chugg. **90:** Alexander and Porus © Andrew Michael Chugg. **98:** Mallian wall © Andrew Michael Chugg. **100:** Gedrosian Desert © Andrew Michael Chugg. **102:** Susa weddings © Andrew Michael Chugg. **103:** Opis © Andrew Michael Chugg. **104:** magi/Braun and Schneider/used with permission by C. Otis Sweezey. **116:** Roxane and Alexander IV © ARTOTHEK. **119:** Zoroastrians © Mohammed Kheirkhah/UPI/Landov. All public domain images and other photos from royalty-free stock sources are not credited.

◂ CONTENTS ▸

A

Introducing...
The Superman of
the Ancient World

*There is nothing impossible
to him who will try.*

—ALEXANDER THE GREAT

A

When Alexander was sixteen, his father left town on business for a month and put him in charge—not of the house, of the *whole country*. See, Alexander's dad was king of Macedon, a powerful city in ancient Greece.

Ruler for a month? The opportunities must have boggled young Alexander's mind. Should he ban schoolwork? Race chariots through the palace halls? Create new laws just for fun? Nah. Alexander wanted something bigger. And he got it when a barbarian tribe attacked the borders of his kingdom. Like Superman trying on his cape for the first time, Alexander flew into action, ordering his father's men to follow him into battle.

Here's the weird part: They did.

Hordes of grizzled, bearded war veterans streamed into formation behind their baby-faced leader. They could have said, "Look, we'll start following you after you start shaving." But they didn't. Even as a teenager, Alexander dazzled the men with his leadership powers. They unquestioningly backed him up as he defeated a rebelling tribe from Thrace, conquered their capital, and renamed the city after himself—Alexandropolis. The kid had nerve on and off the battlefield.

Alexander's first victory launched his rise to greatness. Less than two years later, at age eighteen, he led the army as their general. By twenty, he ruled over all of ancient Greece, and by twenty-five, he had conquered most of ancient Persia (today's Middle East). In thirteen years of fighting, he never lost a *single* battle.

By the time he died at thirty-two years old, Alexander was King of the World.

More importantly, Alexander unified his kingdom with a common language, a common currency, and an uncommon respect for diversity. In those days, ancient conquerors usually forced their subjects to give up their religion and customs. Not Alexander. He was twenty-four hundred years ahead of his time. He respected other cultural traditions and brought leaders of all faiths into his inner circle—and the results were historic. By mixing the best of Greek and Middle Eastern cultures, Alexander ushered in one of the most exciting and creative periods in ancient history. Historians call it the "Hellenistic" age.

Yet one of Alexander's greatest ironies is that he tried to achieve worldwide peace and brotherhood through warfare and bloodshed.

What drove Alexander to conquer the world? And where did he get his progressive ideas of religious tolerance and respect for cultural diversity?

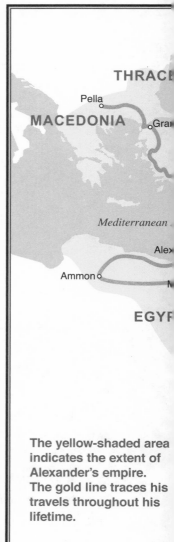

**The yellow-shaded area indicates the extent of Alexander's empire.
The gold line traces his travels throughout his lifetime.**

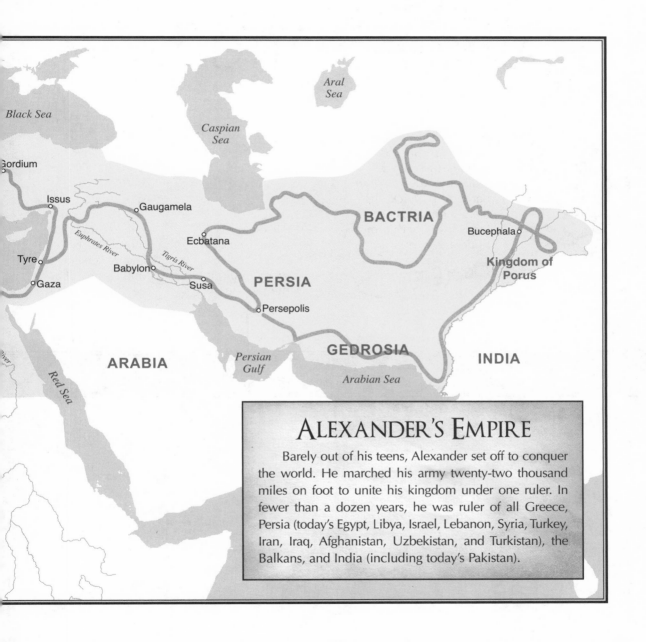

Black Sea

Aral
Sea

Caspian
Sea

Gordium

Issus

Gaugamela

BACTRIA

Bucephala

Ecbatana

Kingdom of
Porus

Tyre

Euphrates River

Tigris River

Babylon

PERSIA

Susa

Gaza

Persepolis

ARABIA

Persian
Gulf

GEDROSIA

INDIA

Arabian Sea

Red Sea

ALEXANDER'S EMPIRE

Barely out of his teens, Alexander set off to conquer the world. He marched his army twenty-two thousand miles on foot to unite his kingdom under one ruler. In fewer than a dozen years, he was ruler of all Greece, Persia (today's Egypt, Libya, Israel, Lebanon, Syria, Turkey, Iran, Iraq, Afghanistan, Uzbekistan, and Turkistan), the Balkans, and India (including today's Pakistan).

IMPORTANT DATES OF · ALEXANDER THE GREAT ·

Alexander is born.

AGE 16:
Alexander runs the country for his dad while he's away. When barbarians attack, the teen commands and leads his father's army to defeat them.

AGE 20:
Alexander is named King of all Greece when Philip is murdered.

AGE 23:
Alexander "solves" the riddle of the Gordian Knot. Later he defeats Persian King Darius III at the Battle of Issus.

356 BCE	343 BCE	340 BCE	338 BCE	336 BCE	334 BCE	333 BCE

AGE 13:
Aristotle begins tutoring Alexander.

AGE 18:
Alexander is named general.

AGE 22:
Alexander invades Persia. He wins the first battle, the Battle of Granicus.

Talk about Time...

Alexander was born in 356 BCE* (before the common era). BCE years are counted backward, which explains how he was born in 356 but died in 323. Today we count our years forward, because we live CE (in the common era). To figure out how many years ago Alexander the Great was born, add 356 to the current year: 2006 + 356 = 2362 years ago.

* The abbreviations BC (before Christ) and BCE (before the common era) mean the same thing and are interchangeable, as are the abbreviations AD (*anno domini*, or "the year of the Lord") and CE (in the common era).

AGE 25:
Alexander defeats King Darius at the Battle of Gaugamela.

AGE 30:
Alexander defeats King Porus. Later that year he almost dies from an arrow wound in his lung.

AGE 32:
Alexander marries the daughter of King Darius during a mass wedding.

332 BCE	331 BCE	327 BCE	326 BCE	325 BCE	324 BCE	323 BCE

AGE 24:
Alexander is crowned Pharaoh in Egypt.

AGE 29:
Alexander captures rebel holdings in today's Afghanistan. He marries Roxane. He begins the invasion of ancient India.

AGE 31:
Alexander turns back and marches through the Gedrosian Desert.

AGE 32:
Alexander returns to Babylon and dies from a mysterious ailment.

CHAPTER 1

A WILD AND CRAZY FAMILY

For rarely are sons similar to their fathers:
most are worse, and a few are better than their fathers.

—HOMER

A

One day in the year 356 BCE (before the common era), a temple burned to the ground. This wasn't just any temple—it was one of the biggest temples in the ancient world, with columns sixty feet high. And it wasn't in just any city—it was in Ephesus, deep in the heart of Persia, the sworn enemy of Alexander's father and the rest of the Greeks. At the sight of their precious temple in flames, the priests panicked. They ran through the streets, crying and beating their faces. As they slapped themselves silly, they wailed that this ill-fated day marked the beginning of the end of their great empire. And it just happened to be the very day that Alexander III (later called Alexander the Great) was born.

Man, talk about an entrance.

From the beginning, Alexander caused a stir. But nobody guessed he'd end up ruling the known world. Most folks figured that if anyone was going to run the planet, it would be Alexander's father, Philip. He had massive military mojo of his own. In fact, if Philip hadn't fathered Alexander, you'd probably be reading about *him*—maybe as "Philip the Powerful" or (more likely) "Philip the Ugly and Mean." Instead, Philip's fair-haired boy was destined to steal the spotlight—which, of course, would not sit well with Daddy the Destroyer.

THE LAND OF ENDLESS SQUABBLES

To understand Alexander and his father, you have to understand their world. The ancient Greeks may have invented democracy and theater, but that didn't stop them from being savage, unruly, and paranoid. And those were just the citizens. The politicians were even worse.

Folks from sophisticated city-states like Athens looked down on the citizens of Macedon, just as some people in big cities today look down on people "living in the sticks." Athenians liked to build temples, write plays, and make music. The Macedonians? They herded goats, hunted bears, and drank undiluted wine.

Even worse, a king ruled the land. Proud of inventing democracy, Athenians especially detested a single person having total power. They believed that even a "good" king couldn't be trusted; after all, he was only one dagger thrust away from a "bad" king taking over.

The Greek cities operated like our states, which is why they are called "city-states." And although they were all part of Greece—just as all fifty states are part of the U.S.—each followed its own form of government. (Can you imagine what a mess we'd have in the U.S. if each state had a different form of government? What if Massachusetts were a democracy, and California a military state, and Texas ruled by a king? And what if California wanted to take over the western half of the country? Surf's up, Dakota dudes!)

ANCIENT GREEK CITY-STATES

The Greek cities operated like our states. And although they were all part of Greece, each followed its own form of government.

THE LIMPING, ONE-EYED KING

It's safe to say that Alexander didn't get his famous good looks from his father. King Philip was strong, dark, but definitely not handsome. To put it kindly, he looked like a Neanderthal. Battle scars covered his hairy body. He had lost one eye in battle, and he limped

▲ Philip II of Macedon

as a result of a leg injury. But Philip used his awful appearance to his advantage—by scaring people. He looked like someone who would cut you down as easily as look at you.

Philip also tricked people into thinking he was just as stupid as he was ugly. But he was, in fact, a brilliant military leader. He took his ragtag crew of unruly, drunken men and turned them into the strongest, fiercest, most disciplined force Greece had ever seen. Then Philip turned that force on his own neighbors. Power hungry? The man was starving.

In ancient Greece, Athens was a democracy, so citizens voted for their laws and leaders. Other cities, such as Sparta, were run by military governments. Still others, including Macedon, Alexander's home city-state, were monarchies led by kings.

King Philip ruled Macedon in the northern reaches of ancient Greece (today's Balkans), and it wasn't a pretty place. Men guzzled wine out of bullhorns. Boys had to wear rope belts until they killed their first man in battle. Young men couldn't even eat at the "men's table" until they killed a wild boar with their bare hands. Nice, huh?

But, under Philip, the Macedonians kept a lot of the other invading barbarians out of the rest of Greece. The Greek city-states bickered over land and resources like children grabbing for the last piece of candy. All that infighting left them open to invaders. Greeks feared outside domination, but they never guessed that their own neighbor—Alexander's father, King Philip—would be the one to kick their rears into gear.

ANCIENT WARFARE:
YOU COULD PUT AN EYE OUT WITH THAT THING!

Historians credit Alexander's father for (among other things) inventing the *sarissa*, a fourteen-foot-long pike tipped with an iron blade. And, yes, it *was* designed to put an eye out—and a skull and the occasional beating heart.

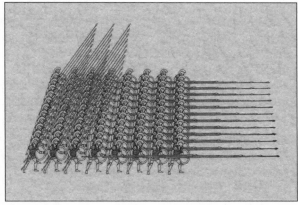

▲ A phalanx

Soldiers used the sarissa while marching shoulder-to-shoulder, front-to-back in a formation called a *phalanx*. Before the phalanx, fighting was a wild rush-to-the-other-side, kill-'em-before-they-kill-you affair. The phalanx changed all that. Fighters had to learn how to hold their sarissas—either straight up while marching or straight ahead while charging. Without that training, soldiers might accidentally shish-ka-bob a friend or get all tangled up with each other. And nobody wanted to die looking like a porcupine on a bad hair day.

A typical phalanx battalion included sixteen groups of 256 men. That's more than four thousand men marching at you, ready to crush your skull before you can even reach for your sword! One look at the wall of death and many soldiers surrendered on the spot.

▲ Greek foot soldier or *hoplite*

Historians believe that Philip also invented the first professional army, as in paid, full-time soldiers. Previously, young men fought for their king "as needed" or were drafted for short periods. Philip paid soldiers to stay soldiers. And they stayed by the thousands.

"WHATEVER YOU CAN DO, I CAN DO BETTER!"

Alexander always wanted to outdo his father. If Dad had a big army, Alexander's would be even bigger. Alexander was especially jealous of Philip's victories. "Boys, my father will forestall [meaning: do it before] me in everything," he complained to his friends as a teen. "There will be nothing great or spectacular for you and me to show the world."

Not quite. Philip only wanted to take some cities in ancient Turkey. Alexander was going to take over the known world.

A SNAKE-HANDLIN' MAMA

Alexander's mother was a powerful force in her own right. Olympias, a beautiful and cunning woman, worshipped Dionysus, the god of wine and wild parties. Deeply devoted to her religion, she handled snakes in ceremonies called "The Mysteries," in which people drank wine and danced on a hilltop under the full moon.

Snakes frightened her husband, Philip, which gave Olympias some evil ideas. She hid coiled reptiles in her clothing and let them jump out and hiss at Philip when he least expected it. *"S–s–s–surprise!"*

Olympias's sneaky "snake attacks" may have been her way of expressing affection. But they also served to remind her husband of an important fact: When it came to playing power politics, Olympias had her own stash of slithering secret weapons.

Alexander's mother was wife number three in Philip's collection of political wives. In those days, kings could marry as many wives as they wanted—often using marriage as a peace treaty. So every time Philip took a new city, he took a new wife. But Olympias ruled the palace as queen. Why? Because she gave birth to Alexander, the only viable heir to the kingdom. Wife number one had a baby boy, too, years before Alexander, but that son ended up with the intelligence of a turnip. Rumors flew that Alexander's mama had poisoned the other child to ensure he would never be smart enough to rule.

Olympias doted on her precious prince, and some suspect she used the snakes to protect him. No doubt, she wouldn't let anything get in the way of her own—er, her son's—ambition to rule the land. There would be no more baby boys after Alexander if she could help it. She would see to that.

IT'S ALL GRΣΣK TO MΣ!

Ω

Different men seek after happiness in different ways and by different means, and so make for themselves different modes of life and forms of government.

—ARISTOTLE

WITH PARENTS LIKE THAT...

We don't have any record of what life was like for Alexander as a baby or young boy, but between his dad's wars and his mom's warpaths, it's no surprise that he grew up to be such a brilliant warrior.

From his father, Alexander learned to fight. And from his mother, he learned to fight dirty.

CHAPTER 2

GREEK BOY WONDER

A hero is born among a hundred,
a wise man is found among a thousand,
but an accomplished one might not be found
even among a hundred thousand men.

—ARISTOTLE

B

Even when he was just a kid, Alexander showed a talent for tricking his enemies—but not with a sword. He often used a secret weapon that was much more powerful: sheer charm. The boy could talk a gorilla into handing over its last banana.

At the age of seven, Alexander tricked ambassadors from the King of Persia into revealing key military information. At the time, the Persians were the main musclemen of the world. They were big, powerful, and hungry for more territory. Years earlier they had invaded Greece and even sacked Athens. The Greeks eventually pushed them back, but the Persians were itching for another crack at their western neighbors. They looked at Greece the way a hungry wolf looks at a squirrel. (*Mmmm, lunch!*)

When the ambassadors arrived in Macedon, they discovered that the powerful King Philip was out. They were totally disappointed. Now how could they find out what Philip was up to? Frustrated over making such a long and fruitless journey, they couldn't resist the little fair-haired, gray-eyed prince who invited them to sit down. And they didn't refuse Macedonia's famously strong wine, either. Reclining on the Greek couches, the men began to relax. That's when Alexander started asking questions.

He wanted to know "the nature of the journey into the heart of Persia" and the "King's experience in war." Was the Great King of Persia a strong fighter? How many warriors did he have in his army? What kinds of weapons did they favor? How were the men trained?

Charmed and flushed with wine, the men answered all of Alexander's questions, probably giving away more information than they intended. In fact, the ambassadors later claimed they were "filled with admiration" for the boy—which is, if you think about it, a little like telling a cobra you "admire" his fangs. More than fifteen years later, Alexander's forces destroyed the armies of every man who was in the room that day.

HOLD YOUR HORSES!

Like most boys in Macedonia, Alexander loved horses—and he could probably ride one before he could walk. When Alexander was about nine, he joined his father to examine some warhorses for purchase. One caught the boy's eye—a shining black stallion. But nobody could get near the snorting, angry beast. It bucked every rider who tried to mount him and fought the groom trying to hold him.

So, of course, Alexander wanted *that* one.

But Philip told the sellers to take the horse away. Alexander couldn't believe his father was going to give up such a magnificent animal for his men. "What a horse they are losing," he burst out. "And all because they don't know how to handle him!"

Philip turned to his son and arched a brow. "Are you finding fault with your elders because you think you know more than they do or can manage a horse better?"

"At least I could manage this one better!" Alexander shot back.

Philip glared at his son. "And if you cannot, what penalty will you pay for being so impertinent?"

▲ The taming of Bucephalas

"I will pay the price of the horse," Alexander claimed proudly. Everybody laughed. The horse cost the equivalent of several hundred thousand dollars. But Philip agreed.

Alexander approached the stallion. As he got closer, he made an important discovery. The horse wasn't angry. It was scared—spooked by its own shadow in the bright sunlight. Before it could jump again, Alexander grabbed the bridle and turned the horse to face the sun. Now that the stallion's shadow fell behind it, would it still spook? The horse struggled at first, shaking his head and neck, but Alexander held on. He began to whisper soothingly in the horse's ear. The stallion calmed—for the moment anyway. Then with a single leap, Alexander jumped onto the horse's back. But instead of rearing, the horse bolted with such a burst of speed that everyone watching moved back out if its way.

The horse handlers groaned. Having their wildest horse take off with the king's son did not bode well for sales—or their heads. If something happened to the boy . . . well, they didn't even want to think about it. Everybody in the ring was in an "agony of suspense." What if the horse started bucking? Even if it didn't, could Alexander control the horse and make it come back?

Just as King Philip was about to call for his own royal mount to chase the boy down, he saw Alexander cantering into view. Slowly. Confidently. And with a big grin. He had done it! Alexander had tamed the wildest horse of the lot. Everybody cheered with relief (especially the horse handlers).

Philip almost wept. When Alexander dismounted, he grabbed Alexander by the ears and kissed him on the forehead. "My son," he said, "the horse is yours. But you'll have to find another kingdom. Macedonia isn't going to be big enough for you."

It's almost as if his dad had a crystal ball or something.

A WARRIOR...PONY?!

Greek horses were quite small by today's standards. In fact, the "beast-like" Bucephalas probably was not much bigger than a pony. How do we know? In one account of Alexander's army crossing a river, the narrator explained that the water reached the men's chests, but the horses struggled to keep their heads above water.

Having a smaller horse was a good thing for another reason: Alexander and his men rode without stirrups. They hadn't been invented yet. Without stirrups for balance, a warrior could easily slip off his horse during battle. Cavalrymen used their legs to control their horses.

▲ Famous statuette of Alexander and Bucephalas

YO, OXHEAD!

Alexander's horse's name was Bucephalas, meaning "ox head," because of his stubbornness. But Alexander loved that horse. He rode him in almost every major battle. In fact, he and his horse were inseparable until the day Bucephalas died. According to legend, Bucephalas never let anyone else ride him. Not only that, but the powerful beast also kneeled for Alexander whenever the young king wanted to jump on.

Once, on a march through foreign lands, horse thieves stole Bucephalas. Bad idea! Alexander flew into a rage. He stomped and fumed and spread the word that if he didn't get his horse back, he would destroy every village within miles. Terrified, the horse thieves immediately brought Bucephalas back. They figured Alexander would jail them, kill them, or enslave them. But Alexander was so relieved to get Bucephalas back that he *paid* the thieves for the horse's safe return. The shocked thieves ran for their lives.

In 326 BCE, Bucephalas died at the old age of thirty. Alexander was crushed. He named a city after his favorite horse: Bucephalia, which was in India, but is in today's Pakistan.

ANCIENT OLYMPICS: KILLER CONTESTS

Warriors in ancient Greece were like today's superstar athletes. People treated them as if they were gods. Greeks wrote epic poems about them and even made sacrifices to them. All that attention went to the warriors' heads. This created a problem during peacetime: No war meant no fans. No fans meant no fun.

The solution? Make some athletic contests to showcase the warriors' skills. Many of these contests actually took place during the funerals of fallen heroes. This makes a lot of sense, don't you think? "Our buddies just died in battle. Quick, let's race to see who's fastest!" Yeah, okay, it may seem odd to us, but to ancient Greeks, racing around the grave of their friend showed the deceased honor and respect. Plus warriors proved their talents in running, throwing, wrestling, and boxing without actually killing anybody. Athletic contests also kept them in shape during peacetime. These competitions grew until they eventually became the Olympic Games.

Unlike today's Olympic events, the ancient Olympics also had a "kid" category. Boys ages twelve to eighteen could compete on the first day of the Games—but only in running, wrestling, and boxing. And, like the men, boys had to compete in the nude. For that reason, girls couldn't even watch the Olympics, let alone participate. Once, a woman was so desperate to see her son compete that she came dressed as a trainer so she could watch him. She got so excited when he won the race that she started jumping up and down. When her disguise fell, the gig was up. So they changed the rules. After that, both athletes *and* trainers had to be in the nude!

▲ Olympic torch relay

OLYMPIAN-SIZED IMPACT

The Olympics may have been around for hundreds of years before Alexander, but it took our boy to turn it into a worldwide party.

The Olympics were originally an all-Greek event, dedicated to Zeus. Athletes competed for the glory of the big guy in the sky, but the riches and fanfare Zeus's followers showered on the winners didn't hurt either.

When Alexander was eighteen, his dad built the Philippeion, a monument dedicated to athletic victories. But instead of placing statues of the gods there, Philip erected statues of himself and Alexander. Some scholars think that's about the time athletes stopped competing for the glory of the gods—and began competing for the glory that came with just plain kicking butt.

As Alexander spread Greek culture throughout the world, the Games attracted athletes from all over, including Antioch (Syria), Sidon (Lebanon), and Alexandria (Egypt). Thanks to Alexander, the ancient Games took on the international flair that our Olympic Games are known for today.

HERE, KITTY, KITTY...

Even as a kid, Alexander loved to hunt wild game. Lions were his favorite. In ancient times, the majestic beasts roamed freely on the Greek peninsula. Several generations of young men showed off their manhood by wearing the skins of lions they'd killed—and, unfortunately, hunted them to extinction. So much for macho.

▲ Alexander and a friend fighting a lion

Alexander pursued his love of hunting, even while conquering the world. Once, in between battles in Persia, he grew restless and invited visitors from Sparta to go on a lion hunt. The Spartans asked Alexander if he were battling the lion to see which would be king. Alexander was in no mood for jokes, though. He tracked a large lion and cornered him. The lion's roar was probably enough to make the Spartans—known as the bravest and most warlike people in Greece—quake in their leather sandals. That didn't stop Alexander. Armed with only a spear, Alexander took down the great beast with one thrust. The Spartans were impressed. To them he acted like the King of the Jungle, as well as King of the World.

JOCK OF AGES

Being a great athlete in the country that invented the Olympic Games was no small thing. Alexander was muscular and strong, and he wielded a mean sword. He was also a very fast runner who loved to race. At twelve, he was encouraged by friends to run in the Olympic Games. He told them he would, but only "if I have kings to run against me."

Why not just run the race? Was he afraid of losing? Or did he think others might "throw" the race rather than beat their future king of Macedon? Nobody knows for sure. But he loved to run, and he carried his love of running into adulthood. For example, on his way to fight the Persians—probably feeling a bit like David in the face of Goliath—Alexander's first stop was the ancient city of Troy. His first act was to race his best friend Hephaestion around the city. Want to guess who won? (Hint: This book is not about "Hephaestion the Great.")

Although Alexander refused to compete in the Olympic Games as a teen, he loved to host contests and races as an adult. After every major battle, Alexander hosted Olympic-like games to celebrate the victory. Running, wrestling, and boxing contests were fun and helped his men let off steam after the stress of battle. But Alexander added something new to his version of the Olympic Games. He held poetry and playwriting contests, too. His bravest warriors could do more than out-wrestle each other to see who was strongest. They could out-write each other to see who was smartest.

ANCIENT SPORTS:
"DUDE, WHERE'S MY UNIFORM?"

Greek boys played team sports that look a lot like today's soccer and dodge ball. Only they played in the nude. (Which makes you wonder—how did they know who was on whose team?) Men—young and adult—competed without clothing because the Greeks thought the male body was perfect. No need to cover up perfection. To protect themselves from sunburn,

▲ Young Greek women line up to race.

athletes coated their bodies with oil and then rubbed on sand, which created a sticky goop. When they finished, athletes scraped off the sweaty gunk with metal scrapers called strigils. A lot of body hair probably went along with them. (Ouch!)

Except in the city-state of Sparta, girls couldn't play organized sports. But they played by themselves. Girls had their own races and played tag, and some ancient vases show them juggling and playing balancing games.

CHAPTER 3

SCHOOL OF
HARD KNOCKS

The roots of education are bitter,
but the fruit is sweet.

—ARISTOTLE

Γ

Poor Alexander. It wasn't enough that his dad wanted him to shine as a great athlete and horseman. Philip also wanted Alexander to be the smartest kid in the kingdom. And that meant schooling—lots of it. Which makes you wonder: What *do* future warrior-kings learn in school? Pillaging 101? Advanced Plundering? Bludgeoning for Beginners?

You might be surprised to learn that Alexander's early education focused on the arts: music, reading, and poetry. But that didn't last long. King Dad wanted a teacher who could prepare Alexander for the real world. Unfortunately, the real world in ancient Macedon was vicious, bloody, and cruel. So Philip looked for the meanest, toughest teacher in the meanest, toughest city-state: Sparta.

MACHO, MACHO MEN

The Spartans were tough. Military training started the day a boy was born. City leaders inspected every newborn, and if they thought a baby looked weak, they left it to die outside the city gates. The mother had no say in the matter. Even worse, kids didn't actually belong to their parents—they belonged to the state. And when kids turned seven, the state dragged them from their homes and threw them into military schools. That's when the real fun began.

▲ Young Spartan warriors-in-training

Teachers made kids swim in cold rivers and march barefoot and naked through rocky mountain passes. (And you thought *your* teachers were tough!) They forced students to box, wrestle, and fight with swords. And, to add insult to injury, the teachers starved them. They *wanted* the boys to steal food from neighboring farms—because they figured that a sneaky kid would turn into a resourceful warrior. But if he was caught stealing—watch out! That student was beaten—not for stealing, but for being stupid enough to get caught.

Alexander's teacher was Leonidas, a true-blue Spartan. Forget "no pain, no gain." For Leonidas, the motto was "no sting, no king."

IT'S ALL GRΣΣK TO MΣ!

Ω

The mind is not a vessel to be filled but a fire to be kindled.

—PLUTARCH

LET'S STARVE THE PRINCE

Once Leonidas took over, Alexander's day started at dawn with a several-mile march—or jog—around the palace. Then the Spartan master spent hours training the boy in the fighting arts: spear throwing, wrestling, sword play, and archery. Leonidas also drilled Alexander on military techniques and strategies and made sure he kept up with his reading and writing. Whenever Leonidas was unhappy with Alexander's performance, he sent the boy on another long march in the evening, this time without any food. And Alexander was only seven!

Years later, Alexander told one friend that to Leonidas, breakfast was "a long march and dinner a light breakfast." His mother must have worried, because she tried to smuggle treats into his room. But Leonidas went through Alexander's things, throwing his clothes on the floor and rifling through his trunks. Alexander hated the lack of privacy.

Maybe nobody told Alexander that Leonidas expected him to steal food, or maybe he just refused to do it. Either way, Alexander grew more and more hungry—especially for revenge.

"I'LL SHOW YOU!"

Alexander especially hated the way Leonidas yelled at him during morning prayers. Once Alexander grabbed two handfuls (instead of two pinches) of incense and tossed them into the fire, and Leonidas flew into a rage. "When you've conquered the countries that produce these spices," Leonidas thundered, "you can make as extravagant sacrifices as you like. *Until then, don't waste it!*"

Fifteen years later, Alexander *did* conquer the spice-bearing regions in the East. And one of the first things he did was ship eighteen tons of incense to his old taskmaster. Just imagine Leonidas waking up to find his yard filled with dozens of pack mules loaded with spices, eating all of his grass. With the incense was this note: "I have sent you plenty of myrrh and frankincense, so you need not be stingy towards the gods any longer." Signed, the King of All Greece and Persia.

Despite the jab, Alexander came out smelling sweet—he had made his old teacher a very rich man. The incense was probably worth millions.

ANCIENT KIDS: "No, Really! I'll Be Good—I Promise!"

Kids in ancient Greece went to school, competed in sports, listened to music, and played board games. If you think that sounds a lot like your life, think again.

Only rich boys could go to school. (Forget it, girls.) Only boys could compete in sports—and playtime had to wait until a guy had finished all his work on the farm or in the family business. But life wasn't all sweat and toil. All educated kids learned a musical instrument—usually the lyre or flute. And most kids loved to dance, which they did often. Kids also played board games, such as checkers or "knucklebones," a game that used dice made of the anklebones of small animals.

But life was extremely difficult—or even dangerous—for some children. Slaves, including slave children, made up as much as thirty-five percent of the population in the ancient world. Some kids were born into slavery, and others were forced into it after being captured in war. Believe it or not, some children were actually sold into slavery—by their parents! Imagine your folks having *that* choice when you forget to clean your room!

"HONEY, ARISTOTLE'S AT THE DOOR . . ."

By the time Alexander was thirteen, the young prince was a muscular, athletic boy. He could handle the warrior half of being a warrior-king. But what about the king part? Would he know how to make the best decisions? Philip wanted Alexander to be smart as he was strong, so the king went shopping for a new teacher. And he set his sights on one of the greatest minds of the ancient world: Aristotle.

▲ A bust of Aristotle

Aristotle had been teaching at the prestigious Academy in Athens under his famous teacher, Plato. When Plato died, Aristotle thought he would get the top job at the Academy. But he didn't. Instead, Plato's nephew got the spot, proving that even in ancient times, it's not *what* you know but *whom* you know. Disappointed, the forty-year-old philosopher needed a new gig.

Philip reached him by letter and asked him to come to the palace and tutor Alexander. Aristotle was uncertain. How could he work for a king when he believed in democracy? Philip tried to entice him with a lot of gold. Aristotle still hesitated, so the king promised to rebuild his hometown. (Never mind that Philip's own army had destroyed it.) In the end, Aristotle agreed, figuring that although he couldn't stop Alexander from being king, he might at least be able to teach him to respect democracy.

Being tutored by Aristotle would be like having Albert Einstein drop by to teach you science. Who could handle *that* kind of pressure? But it didn't faze Alexander for a minute. It's almost as if he thought smart "aleck" should have been spelled with an *x*.

ARISTOTLE SAYS...

Change in all things is sweet.

We are what we repeatedly do. Excellence, then, is not an act, but a habit.

Hope is a waking dream.

We make war that we may live in peace.

Happiness depends upon ourselves.

"You're Not the Boss of Me!"

Aristotle had his hands full with Alexander. Philip described his son as "self-willed." He was bright, the king wrote to the philosopher, but "very difficult to influence by force." That's a nice way of saying, "He won't do what I tell him!" On the other hand, Philip pointed out, Alexander was also "easily guided by an appeal to reason." Good thing—because Aristotle was the king of "reason," especially a way of thinking called logic. We still use Aristotle's logical reasoning for scientific thinking today.

In the Gardens of Midas

Aristotle and Alexander spent three years at a villa called the Gardens of Midas, a peaceful place with lush vineyards and shady walkways. Aristotle taught most of his lessons outside. Together the teacher and student opened bird eggs to study how chicks were born, dug in the ground for bugs and worms to classify them, and hid in the brush for hours to observe animal behavior.

As the son of a doctor, Aristotle also shared his extensive knowledge of medicine with Alexander. Alexander made good use of that knowledge later. He often treated his own men while on military campaigns. Years later in India, Alexander relied on Aristotle's training to find a cure for a friend in agony from a poison-tipped arrow. The poison caused numbness first, "then sharp pains followed, and convulsions and shivering. The skin became cold and livid, and bile appeared in the vomit, while a black froth was exuded from the wound and gangrene set in."

Recalling his botany lessons, Alexander went on the hunt for a plant cure. He found one that he thought might help, so he ground it up and plastered it over his friend's infected body. Then he made a tea from the plant, which he made his friend drink. The man completely recovered, and Alexander ordered that the remedy be used on all his affected soldiers.

Aristotle would've been proud.

ANCIENT THINKING:
WHY DID ARISTOTLE CROSS THE ROAD?

Because there was something on the other side he hadn't studied yet. The great philosopher Aristotle wrote between five hundred and one thousand books on an amazing range of topics—from biology, physics, music, and geometry to economics, ethics, medicine, and astronomy. Many of these subjects didn't even exist before Aristotle turned them into "sciences."

But Aristotle is most famous for inventing logic—in particular, a type of logical thinking called *syllogism.* A syllogism includes two premises, or statements, and a conclusion (If *x* and if *y* then *z*). Here's his most famous syllogism:

1) If . . . every Greek is a person.
2) And if . . . every person is mortal.
3) Then . . . every Greek is mortal.

Now you know whom to blame for word problems.

Thanks to Aristotle, Alexander became a lifelong learner. In his journeys around the world, Alexander collected plants and animals and sent them back to his old teacher—who then wrote about them in his many books. Alexander even banded a herd of deer, hoping to learn about their migration habits, long before anyone ever heard the word "conservation."

Which only proves . . .

1) If . . . great teachers inspire lifelong learning.
2) And if . . . Aristotle's pupil, Alexander, became a lifelong learner.
3) Then . . . Aristotle was a great teacher.

Pretty logical, huh?

ALEXANDER THE . . . BOOKWORM?

As much as Alexander appreciated science, he treasured stories more. The bloodier, the better, too. And nothing was bloodier than Homer's *The Iliad*. Alexander loved the tales of the Trojan War—stories of adventure, bravery, loyalty, and heroism. He worshipped Achilles, the bravest, strongest fighter of all the Greeks.

Aristotle copied the *The Iliad* for Alexander and included his personal notes. For years Alexander

▲ One story of the Trojan War describes how Greek soldiers sneaked into the city of Troy by hiding inside a giant wooden horse.

carried it in a jewel-encrusted box throughout Persia and India. Amazing, isn't it? With all of the world's treasures at his fingertips, Alexander's most prized possession was an old book.

ANCIENT SCHOOL: SLACKERS BEWARE

School in ancient Greece was no picnic. Students learned to write on a wax-covered board—and the teacher never believed a kid when he said the sun melted his homework. He had to read Homer. Not Simpson, but the other Homer—the epic poet who believed if anything was worth saying once, it was worth saying several dozen times.

Even worse, the family sent the boy to school with an older male slave—called a *pedagogue*—who shadowed the kid's every move. If he slacked off, watch out. Mr. Pedagogue

▲ A bust of Homer

had full permission from Mom and Dad to slap Junior around until he straightened up.

Losing your recess doesn't seem so bad now, does it?

LIKE A FATHER

Alexander claimed he loved Aristotle as much as his father. "One had given him life," Plutarch credits Alexander with saying, but Aristotle "taught him how to live well." Aristotle taught the young prince how to rule well, too. He trained Alexander to analyze his options and think on his feet, both critical skills on the battlefield and on the throne. Aristotle also instilled in his pupil a respect for democracy. (Which is kind of funny—a king who valued democracy?) As a result, Alexander often supported democratic forms of government in the Greek city-states he freed from the Persians.

▲ Aristotle training Alexander

But Aristotle's cheerleading also had a dark side. Aristotle believed that non-Greeks were "barbarians"—that they weren't any better than animals. He told Alexander to rule non-Greeks with an iron fist. But Alexander didn't agree. He treated other cultures with respect. The young king quickly learned that ignoring his teacher would yield powerful results.

After three years under Aristotle, Alexander got new orders. Philip thought it was time for Alexander to stop attacking the books—and to start attacking their enemies. Philip called him home and sent Aristotle packing. Sixteen-year-old Alexander was about to be put to the test—on the battlefield. And for Alexander, this test had only two options: pass or fail.

IT'S ALL GRΣΣK TO MΣ!

Ω

The difficulty is not so great to die for a friend as to find a friend worth dying for.

—HOMER

ANCIENT LITERATURE:
THE ILIAD AND ALEXANDER'S IDOL

THE CRYBABY HERO

What's the difference between Achilles—the greatest hero of all the Greeks—and a puppy? Eventually, the puppy stops whining. (Okay, so it's an old joke. But it's still true!)

Believe it or not, the hero of *The Iliad* whined, pouted, and cried more than a kid who's lost his TV privileges. So why did Alexander idolize him? (Clue: It wasn't because of his great personality.) Everybody worshipped Achilles because he was the biggest, best, and strongest fighter of all time—everyone knew he was invincible. His mother was a goddess who had dipped him in magic water when he was an infant, making him  indestructible (although it didn't stop him from acting like a drip). Enemy armies groaned when they heard Achilles was in the lineup. So what if he acted like a big baby? The only thing that mattered was his amazing ability on the battlefield. Hey, we treat today's sports stars the same way. We overlook their mistakes—even really big ones—as long as they dazzle us with their talent.

THE STORY

Homer's epic story—full of action, adventure, Greek gods, love, jealousy, death, victory, and loss—begins in the tenth year of the war between the Greeks and the Trojans. One of the Greek kings took a prize that Achilles thought belonged to him: a woman named Briseis. So Achilles did the mature thing—he threw down his spear, crossed his arms, and refused to fight. Everybody begged him to go out and smite some more Trojans, but he wouldn't even peek out of his tent.

Without their hero, the Greeks began losing the war. Achilles' best friend, Patroclus, put on Achilles' armor, hoping to trick his discouraged Greek brothers into thinking their hero was back. But during a battle, the Trojan prince, Hector, killed Patroclus, thinking he was Achilles. When Achilles heard what had happened to his friend, he went on a rampage, swearing at the gods and slaughtering anything that moved. He killed Hector, mutilated his body, and refused to let the Trojans bury him (which was a major insult in ancient times).

▲ Achilles bandaging the arm of his best friend, Patroclus

Furious at Achilles' temper tantrums, the gods arranged to have him killed by directing a poison arrow to his one weak spot—the heel by which his mother had held Achilles when she dipped him. (That's why, even today, you might hear people call a weak spot or weakness an "Achilles' heel.")

TWO PEAS IN A GREEK POD

Alexander dreamed of being the next Achilles. He even thought that he had descended from Achilles' line. At least, that's what his mother always told him. Either way, Alexander wanted to be just as brave, strong, and powerful as the greatest Greek warrior of all time.

He almost succeeded. In fact, the similarities between the two are downright eerie. Each led armies as a teenager, was the best warrior of his era, and had a best friend who died before him. And each man took his last breath when he was barely in his thirties.

▲ Achilles and Ajax playing a game, probably dice

The story of *The Iliad* suggested that every warrior should try "to be the best and bravest." Achilles and Alexander lived by that motto—and died by it, too.

CHAPTER 4

TEENAGE GRECIAN HEROIC WARRIOR

*How great are the dangers I face
to win a good name in Athens.*

—ALEXANDER THE GREAT

Δ

What would you say if someone forced you to leave school and plunge into combat with wild-eyed, club-carrying, blood-crazed barbarians?

All right. Now what would you say that we could print?

Alexander's response: *It's about time!* Alexander couldn't wait to prove himself on the battlefield. His hero, Achilles, led an army at age fifteen. At sixteen, Alexander wasn't getting any younger, and, as much as he loved Aristotle and learning, he loved fighting alongside his father even more. After all, the family that slayed together stayed together.

Alexander couldn't get enough of the excitement, the camaraderie, and the victory of battle. Ancient combat was messy, loud, and confusing. And that was just getting the armor on.

On the battlefield, it was murder. Dust from thousands of tramping feet clouded warriors' eyes, the sounds of clanging swords mingled with the moans of the dying, and blood mixed with sweat made it tough to hang onto the thick, heavy weapons.

He lived for fighting—and sometimes he had to fight to live. But more than anything, Alexander thrived on being the hero.

ANCIENT WARFARE:
WEAPONS OF MESSY DESTRUCTION

Ancient warriors may have fought for glory, but their weapons were made to make the fighting *gory*. Here's a sampling of the weapons and equipment Alexander's army used:

- *Sarissa*. Only phalanx fighters used King Philip's famous invention. The sarissa's iron spearhead, shaped like a knife, was set on top of a fourteen- to sixteen-foot-long wooden pole. The spearhead was so heavy that the pole required a counterweight at the other end. Without it, soldiers couldn't even lift the weapon.

▲ A Macedonian phalanx armed with sarissas

- *Kopis*. This sword had a single-edged, slightly curved blade and was mostly used by foot soldiers, who were called *hoplites*.

▲ Kopis

- *Javelins and spears*. Alexander's cavalry carried heavy, long spears as well as swords. Alexander also put archers and javelin throwers on horses to protect the sides of his phalanx.

▲ A vase depicting hoplites armed with spears

▲ A statue of Athena, the Greek goddess of war, with a spear

- *Armor or cuirass*. Alexander's fighters on the front lines wore metal-plated chest and stomach armor called *cuirasses*. But only the officers and key fighters got the ones with the ripped muscles (the first super-hero costumes, perhaps?) The idea, of course, was to scare the enemy—to make them think they were up against a sea of muscle-bound, pumped-up he-men. Soldiers in the middle of the phalanx weren't as lucky—they had to wear armor made of cloth or thickly woven linen cuirasses. And the poor saps in the back got nothing.

▲ Cuirass

- *Greaves*. Front-line fighters also wore *greaves*, a kind of metal shin protector that covered the front of the legs from knee to ankle and were held together with straps in the back.

- *Shields*. Almost all soldiers carried round Macedonian shields. They carried them by straps and held them to the left sides of their bodies, moving them to the front as needed. When Alexander crossed from Greece into Troy (ancient Turkey), a priest presented him with

▲ Greaves

"Achilles' Shield," an elaborately carved beauty that Alexander proudly wore in battle. It saved his life more than once. Of course, it wasn't *actually* Achilles' shield. (Or *was* it?) According to *The Iliad*, after Achilles was killed, Athena offered his armor in a contest. Odysseus, the crafty

▲ A rendering of Achilles' shield

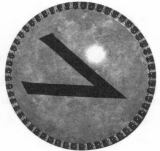

▲ A Spartan shield

trickster, won it over Ajax, the big lug. Then Odysseus promptly lost it. Alexander believed he had Achilles' mythic shield, and it gave him even more confidence than he had before—if that's possible.

ALEXANDER TO THE RESCUE!

In one furious battle with yet another band of barbarians, Alexander's father found himself in trouble. Attacked from all sides, Philip began to weaken. Suddenly an enemy fighter cut Philip deep in the leg. He fell to the ground, slashing wildly as he collapsed. According to Alexander, Philip then pretended to be dead in order to save himself. So Alexander (the hero!) rushed over and protected his father's body with his shield while fighting off attackers with his sword. Alexander saved his father's life—and the day.

Philip never publicly acknowledged Alexander for the brave deed, but he did name him general soon after. Today, you're lucky if you make general before you're fifty. Alexander was eighteen.

▲ A bust of a young Alexander

A REAL TEST

During Alexander's late teen years, his dad went on a rampage to unite all of Greece. With Alexander at his side, Philip threatened, invaded, and conquered all of the major city-states, including Athens. For the first time in their history, one man ruled all of Greece. Not everybody liked this idea—especially powerful politicians in Athens and Thebes, two of the most powerful Greek city-states. Soon after Alexander earned his generalship, the citizens of Thebes decided they didn't like having Philip as their king. So they told him to take a hike.

IT'S ALL GRΣΣK TO MΣ!

Ω

And what he greatly thought, he nobly dared.

—HOMER

They should have known better. Challenging Philip was like waving the green flag at the Indy 500—it was just a matter of time before somebody got flattened. And Philip, with his superior army and superhero son, didn't waste any time marching down to Thebes to get his game on.

Eighteen-year-old Alexander led the cavalry—the part of the army that rode on horses. The cavalry usually served as backup. But Alexander, "noted for his valor and swiftness," began using the cavalry as a "shock" unit to attack first and break through the enemy's front lines. Riding on trusty Bucephalas, Alexander led the charge against a troop of elite Theban fighters called The Sacred Band.

▲ Alexander and Bucephalas

The Sacred Band was like an all-star team of professional players (only without the free agents, pouting, and multi-million-dollar contracts). They were the best of the best: brutal, brilliant, and undefeated. More importantly, each fighter swore to fight to the death rather than lose.

Alexander knew their reputation—and their promise—and neither one disturbed him a bit. The teen general charged into the fray with a war cry that made grown men whimper. Ancient historians give no details of the battle, except to say that it was vicious and bloody. They do tell us, however, that the outclassed Thebans sounded a retreat. All but The Sacred Band. They weren't about to let Prince Pipsqueak beat them at their own game.

But by the time the dust settled, only Alexander and some of his men were left standing. They had done the impossible. Alexander's unit had destroyed the most elite fighting force in all of Greece.

Alexander decided to create his own elite unit: the Companion cavalry.

GREAT IDEA—I THINK I'LL STEAL IT

If imitation is the sincerest form of flattery, then The Sacred Band was flattered to death. Their bravery in the face of defeat so impressed Alexander that, to honor their memory, he erected a giant lion statue where the men of The Sacred Band had died. (You can still

▲ Pairs of soldiers in The Sacred Band protected each other to the death.

see the statue today in Chaironea, Greece.) Then he stole their concept.

Alexander created his own special band of fighters. Like The Sacred Band, Alexander's new group promised to die rather than lose. But the men in Alexander's band came from the cavalry, not the infantry. How could they get their horses to help them fight to the death? Before every battle, did the soldiers whisper into their ears, "Roses are red, violets are blue. Horses that lose are made into glue"? Probably not. Alexander's men simply had a knack for finding horses as fearless as themselves.

Alexander called his group the Companion cavalry. They remained undefeated for more than a decade.

▲ The lion statue that honors the fallen soldiers of The Sacred Band still stands in Greece.

DING! DONG! THE KING IS DEAD!

He had been training his Companion cavalry for two years when the worst happened—an assassin murdered his father right in front of him. Before Alexander could even react, royal guards surrounded the twenty-year-old prince for protection. Only he wasn't a prince anymore. He was the new king.

As word of Philip's death spread, Greeks from conquered city-states everywhere celebrated in the streets. They finally would be free from Macedonian rule. Rebellions erupted in every corner of the kingdom, and the barbarians started attacking Macedon's borders again. Nobody feared the new young king.

▲ Alexander rides into battle.

To make matters worse, Alexander's advisors showed their true colors: yellow. They urged Alexander to "leave the Greek states to their own devices" and "offer concessions" to the barbarian attackers. But the word "defeat" wasn't in Alexander's vocabulary. He ignored his advisors, called up the army, and quickly crushed the barbarian uprisings all the way up to the Danube River in today's Bulgaria.

But while Alexander was away, his enemies came out to play. The warriors of Thebes—the city-state Philip and Alexander had trounced just two years earlier—decided they wanted a rematch—which is pretty much like a junior-high football team challenging the Super Bowl champions.

What were they thinking?

▲ Alexander was a general and a king by the time he was twenty.

OLYMPIAS, THE QUEEN OF MEAN

An assassin may have plunged a knife into King Philip's heart, but most people think it was his wife and Alexander's mother, Olympias, who masterminded the murder. No one knows if Olympias actually planned Philip's murder, but giving her friends high-fives at the news of his death made people slightly suspicious. To add insult to injury, legend has it that Olympias took the assassin's murder weapon and dedicated it to the god Apollo. You only dedicate things to the gods that you especially cherish.

▲ Gold medallion depicting Olympias, Alexander's mother

What would have been Olympias's motive? Olympias was enraged when Philip married his seventh wife, a teenage girl who was younger than his own son. Worse yet, the girl was pure Macedonian, and if the new bride had a baby boy, chances were good that the "pure-blood" prince would rule over Alexander. So when the girl did indeed give birth to a boy, Olympias took matters into her own hands.

Soon after Philip's murder, Olympias roasted his young wife and new baby to death over an altar fire. Others say she stran-

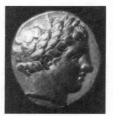

▲ Ancient coin depicting Apollo

▲ Ancient coin depicting King Philip II

gled the baby in front of the mother, and then the mother killed herself afterward. Either way, the message was clear: Don't mess with Queen Mama.

Regardless of the rumors, Alexander believed—as many did at the time—that the Persians murdered Philip. After all, they had found out about Philip's plan to launch an invasion.

HOW BAD A WHOOPING DO YOU NEED?

Alexander tried to talk the Thebans out of declaring war on him. He had always respected them, and he hoped for peaceful negotiations. Besides, didn't they remember how Philip and Alexander's forces had crushed them?

Apparently not. They ignored his attempts at peace and attacked his military outposts near the city. Alexander marched to their city gates and waited to "give the Thebans time to think things over." No go. Thebes sent another group of mounted fighters to attack Alexander, but Alexander quickly checked them. He again asked them to reconsider. Most of the Thebans wanted to avoid war, but a small group of angry officers "urged war by every means in their power." These same officers just happened to be getting bribes on the side from Greece's ancient enemies, the Persians. Greeks claiming they fought for liberty but taking money from the men who were planning to conquer Greece? A funny smell was coming out of Thebes—and it was the stink of double-crossers.

Alexander still hesitated, hoping to avoid conflict, but one of his generals was not so patient. Twitching with anticipation, he attacked without permission, and then there was no turning back. Alexander's superior army flattened Thebes. Afterwards, if you looked up "Thebes" in an ancient dictionary, it would have shown a picture of a hole in the ground—still smoking.

ANY QUESTIONS?

If anybody still doubted Alexander, he wasn't stupid enough to say so. The rest of Greece quickly fell in line. In a matter of months, the young king had subdued all the wild barbarian tribes threatening northern Greece *and* had shut the door on rebellion from powerful Greek city-states. Never before had someone so young done so much in so little time.

But Alexander was only getting started. He prepared to take back the Greek cities the Persians had conquered in western Turkey. Then he aimed to take down the Great King of Persia himself—the man who had paid those Greek officers to revolt against him in Thebes.

This time the Persians had picked on the wrong Greek.

CHAPTER 5

"READY OR NOT, HERE I COME!"

The wise learn many things from their enemies.
—ARISTOPHANES

Ω

You'd think that after proving himself as the unbeatable, undisputed leader of all Greece, Alexander would want to relax a little. You know—kick back, boss people around, count his gold. But not this busy, young king. Friends called the 22-year-old king energetic. But they really meant hyper. The guy couldn't sit still. And after uniting Greece, he had a new obsession—Persia. He wasn't alone. The Greeks, in general, shivered in their tunics whenever the subject of Persian aggression came up. They especially feared the powerful Persian ruler, King Darius III. Why?

Because King Darius served the Dark Lord Sauron and sought the One Ring that would give him power over the hobbits and Middle-earth.

Oh, wait. Wrong story.

Actually, King Darius scared the Greeks because he had built up his armies, reclaimed Egypt after a bloody attack, and was advancing on Greek cities. Remembering how the Persians invaded their homeland years before, the Greeks figured they were next on the take-out menu.

▲ King Darius III of Persia

Not if Alexander could help it. He and his army of forty thousand set off from Greece after King Darius in a pre-emptive attack. Their first stop was the coast of Turkey. Sailing across the channel, Alexander and his men watched silently as the ruins of Troy appeared as they neared the shore. The young king picked up his spear, ran a couple of paces, and hurled it from the front of the boat. The spear, glinting in the bright sun, made a high arc and then pierced the sand with a sharp hiss.

Alexander jumped from the boat and splashed his way to the sand. He grabbed his weapon, thrust it over his head, and shouted that the gods would give him Persia as a "spear-won prize." His men roared in approval.

▲ The lavish city of Babylon was the center of culture, education, and commerce in the Persian kingdom.

BUZZ OFF

Meanwhile, the Great King Darius III lounged in his luxurious palace in Babylon. Despite warnings from military officers, he didn't take Alexander seriously. To Darius, Alexander was nothing more than an annoyance—like a fly buzzing over his soup. Who was this brash young king who dared threaten him? One quick swat with his bejeweled hand, King Darius figured, and he'd be rid of the pest.

So he sent his generals and their forces to head off Alexander. The Persian armies stationed themselves behind a deep, fast-flowing river. Smart move. That meant Alexander's men would have to cross the rushing currents to get to them.

Alexander and his army had been marching since dawn, so they arrived hot and tired at the battle site in late afternoon. They gaped at the seemingly endless line of Persian soldiers stretched along the other side of the river, just waiting to pick them off with arrows and javelins. Some ancient observers estimated that the Persians outnumbered the Greeks two-to-one.

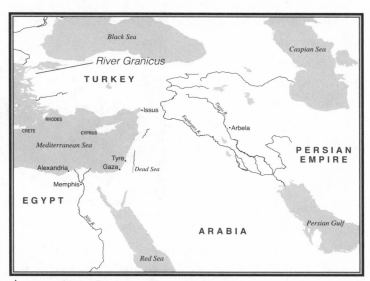

▲ A map of River Granicus in Western Turkey

Alexander's top general urged him to wait. It would be a "grave risk" to attack right then, he said. "The enemy cavalry will fall upon us" and destroy the Greek army. He suggested waiting until dawn. But Alexander had already made up his mind. "I would be ashamed if I could cross [the ocean from Greece] easily," he said, yet have "this mere trickle" of water stop their advance.

That "little trickle" was actually the sixty- to ninety-foot-wide River Granicus (called the Biga River today) in Western Turkey.

IT'S ALL GRΣΣK TO MΣ!

Ω

All virtue is summed up in dealing justly.

—ARISTOTLE

CHAAAARGE!

Alexander leapt onto his horse and led thirteen squadrons of cavalry into the river to start the attack. After battling his way across, he charged the commanding Persian general, who was standing in a large chariot. The general hurled a javelin at Alexander so hard that it stuck in Alexander's shield and almost threw him off his horse. But Alexander "shook off the weapon as it

▲ The Battle of the Granicus was the first of Alexander's victories over the Persians.

dangled by his arm," set spurs to his horse, and thundered toward his attacker. With a savage yell, he threw his own spear so hard that it lodged in the general's chest armor. Men fighting on both sides "cried out" at the force and power of Alexander's attack.

Stunned but not out, the general reached for his sword—but Alexander took the broken javelin still dangling from his shield and slammed it into his enemy's face, finishing him off. At that moment, another Persian fighter charged from behind and cracked "a fearsome blow" on Alexander's helmet, splitting it in two and cutting into his scalp. With blood pouring down his neck, Alexander wheeled and cut down his attacker. Another foe raised his curved sword over Alexander, but one of Alexander's men rushed in and cut off the man's arm in mid-swing.

Soon word spread among the Persian fighters that Alexander had defeated their commanding general. The Persians lost confidence and began to retreat. Alexander's forces pressed and won the day.

King Darius was going to need a bigger flyswatter.

SHARING THE VICTORY

How Alexander acted after the victory tells us a lot about his character—and why his men worshipped him. Despite his bloody head wound, Alexander refused to rest until he had visited all of the injured. He fussed over each man, examined his injuries, and asked how he had received them. He downplayed his own heroism and emphasized theirs. He patiently listened to every story and encouraged each soldier to "exaggerate as much as he pleased." (Locker-room bragging, it seems, was yet another of Alexander's inventions.)

Then Alexander had all of the fallen buried as heroes, which reassured the living. The Greeks believed their souls would not rest without proper burial rites. And to be buried as a hero—well, that meant even the top gods might want your autograph.

Finally Alexander shared his victory with the other Greek city-states. He sent Athens three hundred of the shields that had been captured from the enemy and shipped the spoils of war back home. He picked a few choice objects—fancy drinking cups and elegant wall hangings—to send to his mother.

In the meantime, his nemesis was planning the mother of all get-even battles.

▲ Persian treasures

▲ Greek cup

ANCIENT WARFARE:
THE ERA OF PERSONAL GLORY

Alexander was not your typical he-man-warrior-thug. He was intelligent and cultured. But he was also fearless. Not only did he eventually conquer the known world without losing a single battle, but he also did it at the front of the battle line. Today's military leaders often hunker down in heavily protected, air-conditioned offices miles from the action. Alexander was often the first person his enemies encountered—and almost always the last.

Injuries didn't stop him either. By the time he died, few places on his body were free of scars from arrow slings, sword slashes, or javelin punctures.

Alexander fought during the age of the heroic leader. Everything rested on the top guy. If he felt confident, then his men felt they could win—and fought like it. If he was afraid, his men felt defeated even before the first war cry. Talk about pressure.

Yet Alexander never seemed to be afraid (on the outside, anyway), even when the odds were completely against him. After a while, his legend grew so huge that just the sight of him charging made grown men want to fall to the ground and curl up into a ball.

Alexander dressed the part of the hero, too, in shining armor with two large white feathers, or plumes, on each side of his helmet. He *wanted* everybody to notice him—especially in the thick of battle. After all, how could he inspire his men if they couldn't see him?

Unfortunately, it also made him an easy target for the enemy. Fortunately, the enemy king or general dressed up, too—which also made *him* an easy target. Often these were the battles of the well-dressed, shining heroes.

War is different today. Generals seldom draw attention to themselves, and they rarely speak to an individual soldier. Modern commanders get information by radio, radar, or phone, not by looking around. Alexander would have found this strange—and maybe even a little sad. Where's the personal glory if you're not personally involved?

ALEXANDER AND THE GORDIAN KNOT

After his first victory over the Persians, Alexander made a little detour to the city of Gordium in modern-day Turkey. Legend had it that the famous Gold Meister himself, King Midas, had tied a leather strip to a cart in the middle of the city. The Turkish knot was so complex that nobody had ever succeeded in untying it. In fact, a prophecy emerged that whoever found a way to untie the famous Gordian Knot would rule Persia.

Alexander, as you can imagine, couldn't resist the challenge.

WOULD HE? COULD HE?

Crowds gathered as word spread that the young king was giving it a go. Alexander's generals glowered. What if he failed in untying the knot? Wouldn't that give strength to the enemy? It didn't matter. Alexander had made up his mind, and that was the end of the discussion

After circling the knot for a while, Alexander finally pounced on it. He pushed. He pulled. He yanked. He grabbed. He cursed. The knot just wouldn't budge. In the end, Alexander took his sword, held it over his head, and slashed the knot in two. "I have undone it!" he exclaimed triumphantly.

Well, okay—if you call hacking it off "untying it." King Midas probably had some-

▲ Alexander cuts the mythical Gordian Knot.

thing different in mind. But, then again, nobody else ever had the gall to interpret the challenge that way. Alexander could say he had fulfilled the prophecy: He would rule all of Persia. And after his first performance against Darius's army, nobody dared to argue with him.

"ALL RIGHT, YOU'VE GOT MY ATTENTION"

Losing that first battle made the Great King of Persia sit up and notice Alexander. While Alexander took over more and more Persian territory—freeing the formerly democratic Greek colonies from Persian rule—King Darius pulled together a huge force and set after the boy king. Some historians estimate he had as many as six hundred thousand fighters. Alexander had only forty thousand. Fifteen-to-one odds are not so great.

To his credit, King Darius completely outsmarted Alexander. Well, at first, anyway. Near the Mediterranean coast in present-day southern Turkey, Alexander marched north toward Babylon. But Darius wasn't ahead of him—the Persian king had actually sneaked his huge army *behind* Alexander's forces. (We can almost imagine him thinking, "I've got that wascally wabbit now!") But Alexander discovered Darius's sneaky plan—and did an instant about-face.

He turned his entire army and marched them through the night, just to surprise the would-be surprise-attackers. The next morning, Darius looked up and saw Alexander's army setting up for combat.

Poor guy. Alexander had Darius and his humongous army trapped on a

▲ Remains of the palace at Persepolis, the early center of the Persian empire

narrow coastal plain, hemmed in by mountains on one side and the ocean on the other. In one brilliant move, Alexander had shut the door on the only advantage the Persians had: size. Now they couldn't spread out and overwhelm Alexander's forces. Instead they were trapped like a hundred rats in a shoebox. And the Persians were shaken to the tips of their curved shoes.

ROUND TWO!

Before the next battle, Alexander gave one of his famous pep talks. He reminded his men that they'd already faced danger and had "looked it triumphantly in the face; this time the struggle will be between a victorious army and an enemy already once vanquished." Besides, he continued, "You have Alexander—and they, Darius!" This may sound like bragging, but Alexander knew it would reassure the men because they believed the gods protected their young king.

And it never hurts to have the big guys on your side.

Once again, the Persians had stationed themselves behind a river. But within minutes of the first plunge, Alexander's cavalry demolished the Persian front line. Alexander then set his sights on Darius. Taking him out would not only end the battle, but also finish off the

▲ Alexander addresses his officers before the second battle against the Persians at Issus.

war. He thundered toward Darius, who was waiting for him in his fancy chariot.

Watching Alexander fight his way toward him, Darius must have felt like a dragonfly about to meet his final windshield. His horses, upset by the bloodshed around them, began to rear. Just then another Persian came by with a lighter, smaller chariot. Terrified of being captured, King Darius jumped in and fled.

The Great King of Persia had done the unthinkable: He had run—*run!*—from battle. And he would never live it down.

YOU GOTTA BE KIDDING ME

Alexander fumed. No leader worth his salt ran away from battle! Dying in battle was honorable. Running away was not. Alexander raced after the fleeing king, determined to claim victory once and for all. Just as he set off, he got word that his phalanx was struggling and needed the cavalry's help. Reluctantly, he turned his horse and ordered his Companion cavalry to help out the troops. But the Persians had already seen their great king running away with Alexander giving chase. They lost hope, and the Greeks quickly won.

The entire battle lasted less than an hour.

IT'S ALL GRΣΣK TO MΣ!

Ω

In faith and hope the world will disagree, but all mankind's concern is charity.

—ALEXANDER THE GREAT

▲ This famous mosaic depicts Alexander charging after Darius, who is fleeing from the battle in his chariot.

ANCIENT FRIENDS:
ALEXANDER'S LOYALTY

WHOM DO YOU BELIEVE? Alexander's loyalty to friends was legendary. Once, Alexander's physician and friend, Philip, urged him to take a potion after the young king had fallen sick. But moments before Philip returned with the medicine, Alexander read a note from his top general:

> *Beware of Philip. I am informed that he has been bribed by Darius to poison you.*

When Philip urged him to drink up, Alexander downed the bitter medicine without saying a word. Then he smiled and handed the note to Philip. Philip panicked and begged Alexander to believe that he would never betray him. But the "king's serene and open smile" said it all—Alexander never

▲ Alexander accepts medicine from his physician despite a warning that it is poison.

doubted his friend, which is why he drank the potion before showing Philip the letter.

BEST FRIENDS FOR LIFE. Alexander and his childhood friend, Hephaestion, were inseparable, even as grownups. When Alexander discovered Darius's family had been left behind, he and Hephaestion walked together into the women's tent. The Queen Mother thought that the taller Hephaestion was the king and bowed to him instead of Alexander. A servant pointed out the mistake, and she panicked.

To calm her, Alexander said, "Never mind, Mother. For actually he, too, is Alexander."

FRIENDS IN LOVE AND WAR. Alexander even tried his hand at matchmaking. He discovered a friend trying to sneak home to Greece with a bunch of retiring soldiers. The friend confessed that he was in love with a girl back home and wanted to see her. Alexander made plans to bring the young woman over, telling his friend, "I will help you . . . but you must see whether you can win her either by presents or by courtship." Even in love, Alexander had a plan.

ANCIENT LIFE:
A WAY WITH THE LADIES

Ancient women had it rough. They couldn't vote, hold political office, or go to school. Yet Alexander always treated women with uncommon dignity and respect. He often ordered his men to spare the women in the cities they conquered. And if one of his men mistreated a woman, Alexander usually defended her. For example, after conquering one city, Alexander faced a woman who had been brought to him on the charge of murdering one of his men. The man had attacked her and had urged his friends to steal from her. She tricked her attacker by telling him she had more wealth hidden in a well. When her attacker looked into the well, she pushed him in.

Everybody assumed that Alexander would put her to death. After all, she had killed one of his warriors. But Alexander refused to punish her. Instead he "gave orders that she and her children should be freed and allowed to depart" the conquered city safely.

▲ An ancient Greek woman

Only So Far. Treating women with kindness and respect was one thing; sharing power was another. Despite his respect for women, Alexander never considered letting the Queen of Greece—his mother, Olympias—rule the homeland for him while he was in Persia. Instead he put a man in charge.

Still, his gallant behavior toward women—especially the captured Persian queens—inspired medieval knights. Knights and troubadours sang ballads and told

▲ An ancient Persian woman at work

stories about Alexander's heroics and chivalry. And where did they learn about him? Why, at knight school, of course!

To the Victor Go the Spoils

When Alexander entered his new digs—Darius's abandoned tents—he couldn't believe his eyes. Even the bathtub was made of gold. The young hero turned to his friends and said, "So this, it seems, is what it is to be a king."

Soon after, Alexander discovered that Darius had left more than his belongings. He also left his entire family—including his mother, wife, and daughters. The women wailed in fear before the conquering king, who quickly assured them that he wouldn't hurt them, nor allow anyone else to hurt them. Alexander kept his word. He protected Darius's

▲ Alexander visits the family of Darius III in their tent after the Battle of Issus.

family until the day he died. In fact, the defeated Persian king's own mother became so fond of Alexander that she refused to run away and leave him during a later rescue attempt.

A Little Detour

Amazingly, everything west of the Euphrates River now belonged to Alexander. The young king worked his way down the coastline of modern-day Lebanon and Israel, securing strongholds. After locking up the coast, Alexander had a choice: either face off with Darius one more time or invade Egypt, free it from Persian rule, and claim it for the Greeks. Flip a coin?

He went after Egypt. And that decision would change his life—forever.

IT'S ALL GRΣΣK TO MΣ!

Ω

*A true friend
is a soul in two bodies.*

—ARISTOTLE

CHAPTER 6

EGYPT AND THE FINAL FACE-OFF

Moral excellence comes about as a result of habit.
We become just by doing just acts,
temperate by doing temperate acts, brave by doing brave acts.

—ARISTOTLE

Z

Alexander walked into Egypt a liberator—and walked out a god. Talk about a good day at the office.

See, the Persians had taken Egypt years before and had ruled it with an iron fist. They had sacked the Egyptians' temples, had stolen all their wealth, and had outlawed their ancient religion. The Persians were living large off Egypt's riches. But when Alexander and his army approached, the Persians scurried away like cockroaches when a light's turned on.

The Egyptians threw flowers at Alexander instead of spears because they considered him a liberator. They would accept him as their king in place of the Persians any day.

Besides, the Egyptians had heard that Alexander respected different faiths and religions. When Alexander promised to reinstate their priests and return the right to worship as they pleased, the people fell to their knees in gratitude.

Like a master mummy-maker, Alexander had the Egyptians' hearts and minds all wrapped up.

▲ The Egyptians welcoming Alexander

WE DUB THEE "GOD"

In return, Egyptian priests gave Alexander the title of *pharaoh*, the divine ruler over all of Egypt. Egyptians believed their pharaohs were part-god—which made Alexander a living Greek god. Not a bad rep. Enemies might think twice about attacking a real-life deity. Plus being seen as a god was good for the ego. Maybe too good. After taking over Egypt, Alexander grew obsessed with the possibility of his divinity.

But before he got stuck on that note, Alexander spent time getting to know his new digs. And like a carpenter with new tools, he couldn't resist doing a little remodeling.

▲ A relief in Luxor, Egypt, depicts Alexander as pharaoh.

ANCIENT THINKING:
"I AM A GOD! (AREN'T I?)"

The rumors about Alexander's divinity began early when Alexander's mother, Olympias, hinted that his "real" father was Zeus. Remember how Olympias liked to play with pet snakes? Rumors spread that her favorite snake was actually Zeus in disguise. And Olympias said nothing to squelch the rumors. According to Greek mythology, Zeus often came to beautiful women in the shape of an animal—a bull, eagle, or swan. Why not a snake?

▲ Zeus, the king of the Greek gods

From Hype to Hope. Historians think that Alexander first used the claims about Zeus as propaganda. Enemies were likely to think twice before attacking a son of Zeus. Besides, claiming divinity was common in the ancient world. Persian kings claimed they were gods, and so did Egyptian pharaohs. It wasn't too much of a stretch for Alexander to do the same.

But when did Alexander actually begin to *believe* the hype? Some say it was during his detour to Egypt when he crossed a desert on his way to the famous Oracle of Siwah in modern Libya. As he reached the oasis, the Egyptian high priest welcomed Alexander as the true "son of Zeus." The high priest also announced that the proof of Alexander's "divine birth will reside in the greatness of his deeds." From that point on, Alexander looked at every success as further proof that Zeus was indeed his father.

Over time, his men came to resent the claims. They fought beside their king and saw him sweat and bleed. They weren't convinced. And later when Alexander demanded they bow down to him, they probably grumbled, "Who does he think he is . . . god?"

Well. Yeah.

▲ Alexander laying out ancient Alexandria, Egypt

A CITY IS BORN

Spying some empty land on the edge of the Mediterranean, Pharaoh Alexander imagined a bright and shining city. He "could not wait to begin work [on the city]; he himself designed the general layout." With architects and engineers jogging behind him, Alexander told them where to put the marketplace and even at what angles the streets should run. Finally he told planners to build temples honoring both Greek and Egyptian gods. That was big. Conquering kings usually played the my-god-is-better-than-your-god game and destroyed the native faiths. Alexander seemed to be saying that there was room enough for everybody's beliefs: We can all worship equally.

Meanwhile, Alexander named the city after himself. And why not? Gods could do whatever they wanted. Alexandria in Egypt eventually became the intellectual and commercial center of the ancient world. Scientists, mathematicians, and philosophers flocked to the city. Trade boomed in Alexandria's ports thanks to its giant lighthouse—one of the Seven Wonders of the Ancient World. And its famous library grew to house the largest collection of scrolls and books of ancient times.

▲ The Library of Alexandria was once the largest library in the world.

Today, almost twenty-five hundred years after Alexander founded the city, Alexandria continues to thrive in Egypt. Not bad for a weekend "do-it-yourself" project.

Meanwhile, in what is now Iraq, King Darius had gathered an even larger army than he had led before.

▲ Modern-day Alexandria

And he couldn't wait to get at the young upstart who had humiliated him twice.

Yup. It was time for Round Three.

▲ The Lighthouse of Alexandria was the model for the modern lighthouse.

AND IN THIS CORNER . . .

Alexander marched his army hundreds of miles to meet Darius's forces. Darius had learned his lesson about staying in control of the battleground. This time *he* selected the site—a wide, flat field that would allow him to take advantage of having more manpower. Darius also added two hundred war chariots custom built with sharp blades jutting from the center of their wheels. Like giant lawn mowers, the rotating blades aimed to cut down Alexander's men.

As Alexander's army approached, Darius spread his army out like a snake uncoiling to its full length. When Alexander first spied the massive size of Darius's forces, he could only stare dumbfounded. One ancient historian says Darius had *one million* men to Alexander's fifty thousand. Most modern scholars don't believe Darius had that many men, but they do agree that Alexander was vastly outnumbered.

UH, OH . . .

Alexander's top generals also seemed shaken by the sheer size of the enemy's forces. One seasoned war veteran urged Alexander to attack at night. He reasoned that they wouldn't be expecting an attack then, so maybe the Greeks could gain an advantage.

Alexander refused. He said, "I will not demean myself by stealing victory like a thief. Alexander must defeat his enemies openly and honestly." That meant they would attack at dawn.

But whether Alexander "leaked" word he might attack under the cover of darkness or Darius was just scared that he would, the Persians stayed on high alert all night long. With bows ready and spears high, they waited. And waited. And waited. By the time dawn arrived, the men's "spirit was sapped."

Meanwhile, Alexander went to bed early. He slept so soundly that one of his generals had to shake him awake the next morning. He asked Alexander "how he could possible sleep as if he were already victorious instead of about to fight the greatest battle of his life."

Alexander smiled and said, "Why not? Do you not see that we have already won the battle, now that we are delivered from roving around these endless devastated plains, and chasing this Darius, who will never stand and fight?"

One thing's for sure: Alexander never let the odds get in the way of his optimism.

CONFIDENCE IS CATCHING

As Alexander's warriors prepared for battle, they caught his confident mood. But Darius's sleep-deprived men could only wait nervously. They remembered how Darius had already run away from direct combat with young King Kick-Butt.

As the two armies marched toward each other, Darius ordered his spiked chariots to roll straight into Alexander's front lines. But Alexander commanded his javelin throwers and archers to take out the horses and drivers, stopping the giant mowers in their tracks. However, some broke through. So Alexander gave the order to break formation. His men parted like the Red Sea and the deadly chariots flew through the center without harming a single Greek. Then Alexander's rear guards finished them off.

There would be no human mulch made that morning.

▲ Alexander and his men escaped the sharp blades of the scythe chariots at Gaugamela, the final battle between Alexander and the Persians.

JUST WHERE I WANTED YOU

In a flurry of movement, the armies converged. Slashing furiously, Alexander faked to the right, cut through the center, and blitzed for the ultimate sack—the quarterback, the great King Darius. Again, Darius was waiting in his chariot. As the two leaders locked eyes, everybody knew that the whole future of the ancient world rested on the outcome of the next few minutes.

Darius would either stand and fight or cut and run.

To Alexander's astonishment, he cut and ran. Again.

As soon as the Persians saw their king rolling off, the center collapsed and the Persians retreated. Why should they lose their lives if their own king was making a run for it? It didn't take long for Alexander's army to finish the job.

When the battle was over, Alexander was the new king of all Persia—not to mention the crowned king of Egypt and Greece. Not bad for a twenty-five-year-old.

▲ After escaping from direct battle, Darius was murdered by his own cousin. Alexander came upon the Great King only moments after his death. Many historians think Alexander hoped for a face-to-face meeting so Darius could acknowledge him as "Lord of all Asia." Then he could reinstate Darius as King of Persia but still act as "Over King" of the region.

BABYLON, HERE WE COME!

After his victory, Alexander marched triumphantly into Babylon, the center of the Persian kingdom. He knew, as leaders still know today, that his first act as the new king was a major deal. So what did he do? King Alexander gave orders to restore the temple of Bel—"the god held by the Babylonians in the greatest awe"—which had been destroyed years before when the Persians overtook the Babylonians. Alexander also honored the temples of Mithros, the god of the very people he had just vanquished. Once again, his commitment to religious tolerance earned him the respect of his newly conquered nation.

▲ Alexander and his men entered Babylon through the Ishtar Gate.

Alexander's second act as ruler was to appoint a local Babylonian as governor rather than selecting one of his own Greek officers. Soon after, he chose other Persians and locals to join his governing circle in an effort to build unity among the people.

But Alexander's men hated his ideas of unity. Like Aristotle, they believed that all non-Greeks were merely one step above animals—and should be treated as such. Alexander didn't agree. He soon learned that integration is great in theory, but hard in practice—especially for those who have to share power. The more Alexander integrated local ideas and local leaders into his circle, the more his men grumbled and complained.

Alexander soon discovered that winning back the hearts and minds of his own men was a battle he wasn't prepared for. And, eventually, it was the only one he ever lost.

▲ From a Persian minature painting of *Iskander*, which was the Persian name for Alexander.

WOW! WHAT A GUY!

People flocked to Alexander like moths to a light. They wanted to bask in his confidence, physical strength, and fearlessness. The guy practically dripped charisma.

Alexander's talent for inspiring and motivating others shined brightest before battle. He often rode up and down the front lines, tapping each man's weapon with his own spear and sharing words of encouragement. Remembering the names of almost all of his men, he reminded them of past bravery and invited them to outdo themselves.

▲ Alexander rides down the front lines to motivate his troops.

Like a god in his shining armor, Alexander convinced them they could do even better than they dared to believe. And they almost always proved him right.

THE POWER OF SHARING PAIN

Alexander also had a knack for taking the edge off tough times. He inspired men with his own endurance and his willingness to share their suffering. If they marched through snowy mountain passes, he shivered along with them—even giving away his cloak. If they trudged through deserts, he refused water until they drank first. If they ran out of food, he'd give away his rations and stay hungry until everybody could eat again.

THE MONEY MAN

Money can't buy happiness, but it sure makes misery easier to live with—which is why Alexander paid his men well and gave away almost all of his wealth. After watching him hand out his riches, a friend asked, "But, your majesty, what are leaving for yourself?"

"My hopes!" replied Alexander.

He was even generous with the dead. Or at least with the families of the dead. Alexander honored fallen soldiers by forgiving their families any government debt they owed.

▲ Common coins of Alexander's era

Alexander shared his wealth with the little guy, too. Once, he spied one of his foot soldiers struggling to carry a chest of treasure to headquarters to be counted. Taking pity on him, Alexander cried out, "Don't give up! Finish your journey and take what you are carrying to your own tent." The soldier was allowed to keep the treasure for himself!

Another time he helped a group of former Greek slaves who had been mutilated by their Persian masters. Many had the tips of their noses and earlobes cut off; others had fingers or hands missing. Alexander offered to pay their way back to Greece, but they were too embarrassed to go home. So Alexander ordered a city built for the former slaves and gave them the money they needed to live independently. They would have given everything they had to Alexander at that point—even their right hands (if they still had them, that is).

▲ Alexander caring for Persian women

Finally, Alexander took care of his soldiers' wives and children—both in Greece and in Persia. Alexander swore to educate the children of Greek/Persian unions at his expense—upwards of ten thousand kids. He even created the first army pension, money his ex-soldiers could retire on.

For Alexander, charisma may have gotten the game started, but generosity kept it going.

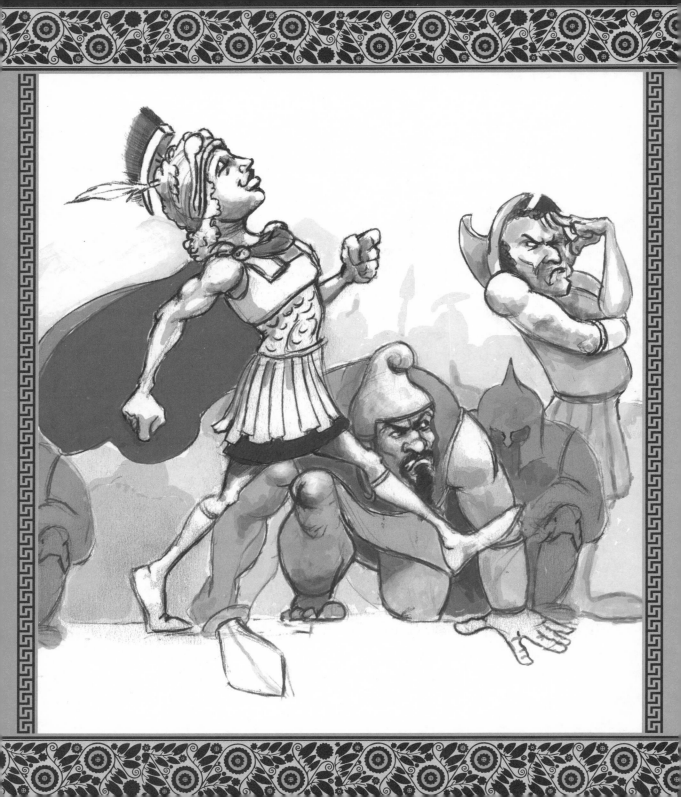

CHAPTER 7

CAN'T WE ALL JUST GET ALONG?

*Justice in the life and conduct of the State
is possible only as first it resides in the
hearts and souls of its citizens.*

—PLATO

It didn't take long for the king of the world to go from hero to zero. His men seethed with resentment over Alexander's attempts at integrating Persians and their customs into his court. Even worse, they felt Alexander had betrayed them by acting "too much" like a king. But wait—wouldn't you expect the king to act like the top guy? According to the Greeks, not if he's your pal.

The problem was a matter of custom (costumes, too, but we'll get to that later). The Persians had a long history of treating their kings like . . . well, kings. For example, a guy didn't look the king in the eye, and he definitely didn't punch him in the arm and joke around with him like a buddy from the neighborhood. The Persians bowed low to the ground in

Alexander's presence—so low that they just about got black-and-blue marks on their heads when he walked past. It was a custom called *proskynesis*. And Alexander liked it. As time went on, he began to think maybe *all* of his people should bow down to him.

Alexander's men recoiled at the very thought.

CULTURE SHOCK

Alexander knew it was a shock for the Persians to have a foreign king. He also knew the importance of their customs and traditions. He wasn't about to tell them that they had to throw everything out the window. So his new subjects continued boppin' their heads on the ground in his presence and, like the Egyptians, claiming he was divine.

▲ A relief depicting *proskynesis*

But his men felt they were treating the king with enough respect if they said "excuse me" when they belched in his presence. Besides, Greeks bowed down only to the gods. Regardless of what Alexander believed about his divinity, his men weren't convinced.

At first, Alexander tried a compromise. The Persians could do their thing when he walked by, but his men wouldn't have to. This might have worked fine, but his men cracked up every time Alexander's new subjects showed respect. And, like most people, the Persians didn't like being laughed at. Meanwhile, Alexander's men accused him of putting on airs by keeping the custom at all.

Alexander couldn't win for losing.

IT'S ALL GRΣΣK TO MΣ!

Ω

*No law or ordinance
is mightier
than understanding.*

—PLATO

DRESSING THE PART

In addition to keeping Persia's royal customs, Alexander began wearing the royal costumes of the land—one more change the Greeks hated. He did this mostly "from a desire to adapt himself to local habits, because he understood that the sharing of race and customs is a great step toward softening men's hearts."

Even so, Alexander only went so far—he refused to wear pants, which all Persian men wore. The Greeks, in their dress-like tunics, thought trousers "unmanly."

Go figure.

But over time, Alexander combined both styles— the fancy robes of the Persians and the casual tunics of the

▲ Variations of the Greek tunic

▲ Examples of Persian trousers

Greeks. At first he only dressed this way among the Persians, but slowly he began to wear the combined outfits in public among the Greeks. Unfortunately, "the sight greatly displeased" his men.

They acted as if their favorite linebacker had just put on a tutu and ballet shoes.

▲ Costume of the Persian nobility

"ARE WE DONE YET?"

But customs and costumes weren't the only reason Alexander's men were angry with their leader. Most of them wanted to go home, but Alexander kept pushing them to secure and expand the kingdom. They also hated his ever-increasing attempts at integration. Alexander took thirty thousand Persian boys and gave orders to educate them for future roles as officers in his army and government. Alexander's men howled in disapproval, calling them Alexander's "ballet soldiers." These boys were being trained to take over their jobs! And it sure didn't help matters when Alexander started calling his officers-in-training the "inheritors."

The Greek officers had no interest in sharing power with the locals. Alexander's army was there to dominate and control, not to share and grow.

What had gotten into this king?

▲ Alexander ordered his officers to train Persians to become part of the military.

WHEN ALL ELSE FAILS, FIGHT!

Meanwhile a nobleman in the eastern part of his new Persian kingdom (today's Afghanistan), rebelled against Alexander's rule. Now *that* Alexander knew how to handle.

Alexander grabbed his forces and marched on the rebels. The insurgent nobleman and his people took refuge at Sogdian Rock, a rough ridge with sharp, sheer cliffs that protected every side. No invading army had ever been able to capture it.

Ever the gentleman, Alexander suggested they give up and avoid a slow, torturous death. Surrender? They laughed down at him, shouting that he'd need "soldiers with wings" to take this rock.

Don't people ever learn?

Hopping mad, Alexander called for his best climbers. Three hundred men showed up at the opening of his tent. He ordered them to climb the unguarded face of the rock—which,

COOL FACT:

Alexander was the last Western outsider to conquer Afghanistan. Nobody has succeeded since. Just ask the British. Or the French. Or the Russians. Or even the U.S. Army.

of course, happened to be the steepest and most dangerous side. He offered them the only tools he had: iron tent pegs, mallets, and ropes.

Oh, and one last thing: They had to climb in the dead of night with no fires or torches to guide them. Today's extreme climbing is a walk in the park in comparison.

Amazingly, all but thirty men made it to the top. Swords drawn, they took their positions directly above the enemy. At the first light of dawn, Alexander told the enemy to look up at the warriors with wings he'd sent to kick their arrogant rears. The rebels stared up into the angry eyes of Alexander's warriors, who were aiming spears and javelins at their heads.

Stunned, they surrendered immediately. Overthrown but impressed, the nobleman later claimed nothing in the world "was impregnable" for Alexander. Little did he know that his own daughter would prove him wrong.

LOVELY LITTLE STAR

At the surrender of Sogdian Rock, many women and children were rounded up with the warriors, including the family of the guy who started the whole thing. That's when Alexander met Roxane, the nobleman's daughter, whose nickname was Little Star. Alexander asked for permission to marry her (instead of commanding her, or taking her, as was his right as king), and they wed right away.

When his men found out that he had married the daughter of a rebel nobleman in a Podunk corner of the empire, they practically coughed up a cow. Was he crazy? Their king should have married someone with power and riches. Or even better, he should have married a noble Greek woman and not a "barbarian." Marry for love? What nonsense!

▲ Alexander weds Roxane.

Still, it was a good move politically. The Persians were "completely won over by Alexander's moderation and courtesy" with Roxane and "encouraged by the feeling of partnership the alliance created."

Now if only his own men could cut him some slack.

HIS OWN WORST ENEMY

Alexander did more than his share of tarnishing his own golden image. He returned his men's distrust with suspicions of his own. And he didn't hesitate to put former friends to death for alleged treason. Plots against Alexander's life hatched faster than eggs in a henhouse.

Then things went from bad to worse. At a drunken party, one of Alexander's old warriors picked a fight with him. Cleitus, "who had already drunk too much and was rough and hot-tempered by nature," began insulting Alexander. Cleitus railed against Alexander, who had also been drinking, accusing him of turning his back on his own father, Philip. Uh, oh. In ancient times, accusations of being disrespectful or neglectful of one's father were right up there with being a mass murderer.

▲ Alexander mourns Cleitus.

"You scum!" Alexander yelled back. "Do you think you can keep on speaking of me like this, and stir up trouble among the Macedonians and not pay for it?"

Oh, they would pay for it. Cleitus explained to Alexander, "But it's the dead ones who are happy because they never lived to see Macedonians . . . begging the Persians for an audience with our own king."

There. He'd said it. They were jealous. They didn't like sharing their king with the Persians.

Cleitus's friends escorted him from the banquet room. But the angry, drunk warrior just came back in through another door and started yelling more insults. In a fit of rage, Alexander threw his spear and pierced Cleitus right through the heart.

IT'S ALL GRΣΣK TO MΣ!

Ω

Remember upon the conduct of each depends the fate of all.

—ALEXANDER THE GREAT

The room went silent in horror.

When Alexander realized what he'd done, he yanked the weapon from the dead man's body and tried to kill himself. His bodyguards stopped him. They forcibly carried the king to his chamber, where he secluded himself in an "agony of remorse." After two days his worried friends forced their way into his room and talked him into putting the killing behind him. He eventually emerged—ready to rule once more.

But murder is murder. Things were never the same again.

ANCIENT MYSTERIES:
DEFEATED BY VICTORY

When did Alexander go from Golden Boy to Tarnished Tyrant? Most historians think Alexander began self-destructing after Egyptian priests "confirmed" his divinity. Others think that the brown-nosing customs of the Persians gave him an insatiable taste for power. Still others think too much drinking led to paranoia and rage.

▲ Egyptian priests

They're probably all correct.

But consider another factor: too much success. Alexander succeeded in everything he had attempted. He didn't lose a single battle in thirteen years of fighting. At a very young age, he became the richest and most powerful man in the known world. Alexander never faced the humbling reality of failure. He believed he was invincible.

Alexander's confidence became his undoing. Like his hero, Achilles, he learned the hard way, proving that death brings even the toughest guys to their heels.

LET'S KISS AND MAKE UP

More than ever, Alexander became determined to create a fusion of customs that everybody could live with. And it all came down to a kiss.

When Persians of equal rank met, they kissed each other on the lips. If one had more authority than the other, the lesser one kissed the greater one on the cheek. If one didn't have any rank at all, he had to do an imitation of a Persian rug and cover the ground. That got Alexander thinking: What if he could prove to his men that he considered them equals yet still have them respect the custom of bowing?

His plan was simple: He invited all of his top men to a party where everybody agreed to share wine, bow to the king, and then kiss him—as an equal. Bowing would prove they were willing to accept Persian customs, while the kiss would demonstrate that Alexander considered them equals.

DON'T KISS OFF THE KING

It almost worked. That is, until one top guy named Callisthenes went for the "kiss of equals" without bowing first. Alexander, who had been talking to his best friend, Hephaestion, didn't notice that the man had "forgotten" to bow. When another officer ratted on Callisthenes, Alexander refused to let him kiss him at all. Callisthenes turned away and said, "Well, then, I must go back to my place one kiss the poorer." The kiss-up had turned into a kiss-off.

Alexander later had him arrested on trumped-up charges of treason. Other men were also put to death for similar "crimes." They began to fear the king they used to adore, and Alexander was no closer to fusing traditions and creating peace with his men than before. In fact, things only got worse.

Alexander's failure at integrating Greek and Persian customs made him yearn for success. So he turned to the one thing he always succeeded in: making more war. But, for the first time in his life, he was leading into battle men who no longer loved and trusted him. And that changed everything.

CHAPTER 8

GAME OVER

A man's character is his fate.

—HERACLITUS

Λ

If Alexander's conquests were like a video game, Alexander's men figured they'd hit the final screen: *Game Over*. After all, they'd marched tens of thousands of miles, defeated their archenemy, and expanded the kingdom. It was time to hang up their shields, retire their joysticks, and head home, right?

Wrong. Alexander had a different message on his inner screen, and it went something like this: *Welcome to Level 2. Ready for more?*

All because he peeked over the side of a mountain.

After taking Afghanistan, Alexander wanted to see the "end of the world," which Aristotle had told him would be right about where they stood on the edge of the Hindu Kush Mountains.

To his amazement, Alexander saw an endless stretch of lush, exotic lands twinkling in the twilight. He gasped—but his men groaned. They knew that wild look in his eyes, the one that screamed, "Mine! Mine! All mine!"

They could forget going home. Their king had found a new obsession.

AN OBSESSION BY ANY OTHER NAME

Alexander looked at India the way a starving man looks at an all-you-can-eat buffet. The Greeks called this kind of fixation "pothos," which means to have an intense desire or violent longing. (If you've ever felt you would just *die* without a new video game or some other "gotta have it," then you know pothos.) Alexander's pet pothos was to keep going and conquer new lands. Unfortunately for his men, they might really die as a result of Alexander's pothos. And they weren't too happy about it.

Even worse, they discovered that the people of ancient India had an obsession of their own: independence.

ANOTHER RIVER?

Alexander's officers feared that their king had gone off the deep end. Just how much power and how much land did he need? And how many of them had to die to help him get it? But nobody had the guts to challenge him.

Alexander and his men fought some of the most brutal battles of their entire careers in ancient India. And they fought at the most miserable time of the year—the monsoon season. Torrential downpours drenched everything. Rust crept over their swords and shields, mold grew on their feet, and moisture rotted their waterlogged clothing. And if the rain weren't bad enough, snakebites killed more men than actual combat.

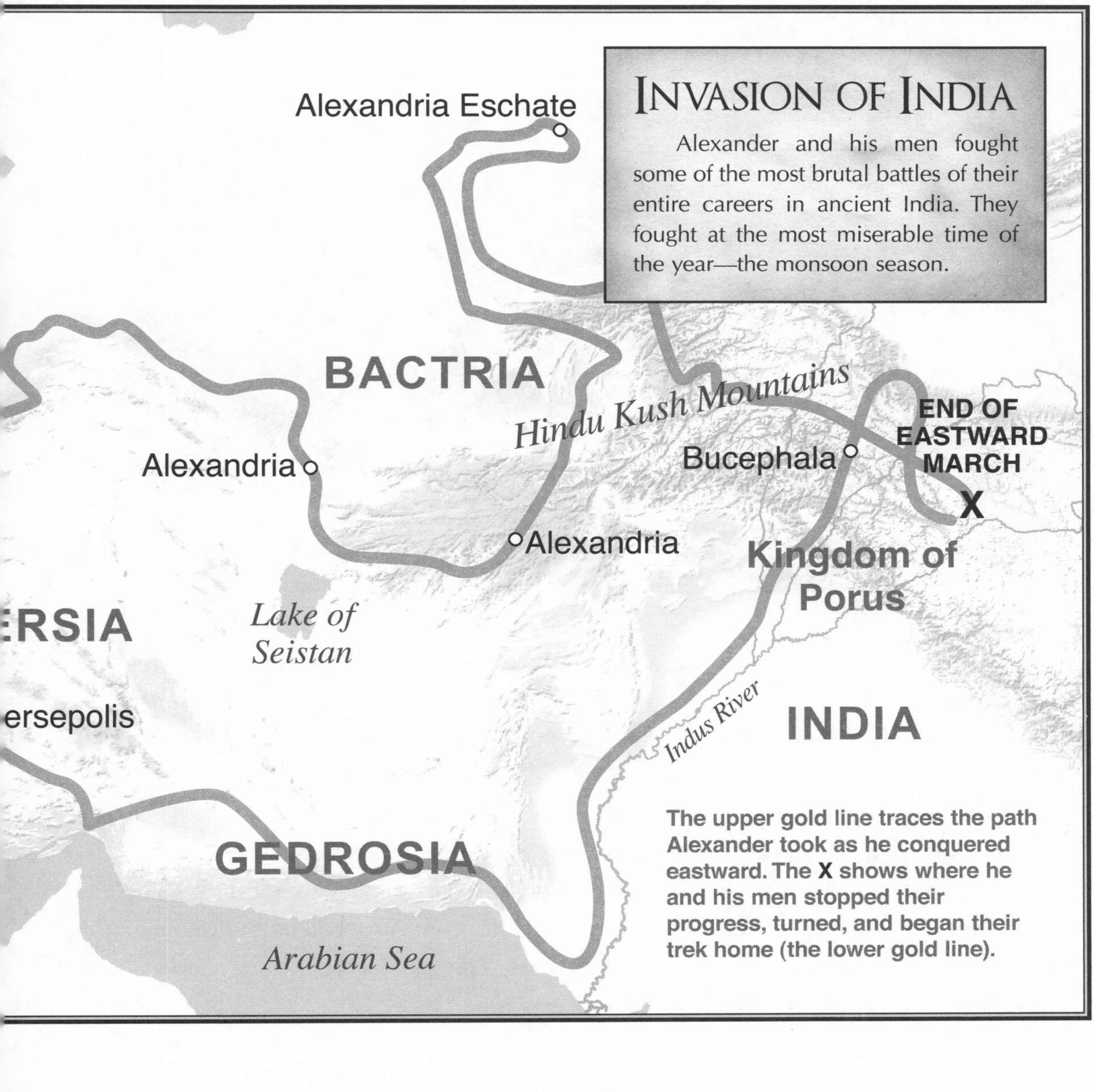

INVASION OF INDIA

Alexander and his men fought some of the most brutal battles of their entire careers in ancient India. They fought at the most miserable time of the year—the monsoon season.

Alexandria Eschate

BACTRIA

Hindu Kush Mountains

Alexandria

Alexandria

Bucephala

END OF EASTWARD MARCH

X

Kingdom of Porus

Lake of Seistan

ersia

ersepolis

Indus River

INDIA

GEDROSIA

Arabian Sea

The upper gold line traces the path Alexander took as he conquered eastward. The **X** shows where he and his men stopped their progress, turned, and began their trek home (the lower gold line).

▲ Alexander accepts the surrender of Porus.

This time Alexander's nemesis was a powerful Indian warlord named King Porus. The rich and powerful Porus led a fierce, well-trained army. Again, Alexander's enemy stationed itself on one side of a churning river. But this time the monsoons made crossing in full view of the enemy too dangerous. Only baffled for a bit, Alexander fell back on his most powerful weapon—his brains. His motto became "if you can't beat 'em, trick 'em."

So day after day, Alexander messed with their minds. He moved large formations of troops to different crossing points. He ordered his men to shout as if they were getting ready to cross and attack. He pretended to launch boats and rafts. Poor Porus had no choice but to scramble into position and rally his men and elephants to prepare for the coming attack.

Which, of course, never came.

JUST KIDDING!

Every time it looked as if the army was launching its attack, Alexander pulled his men back in a "just kidding" retreat. King "Poor Us" fell for it every time. He had to. He couldn't take the risk that *one* of those times Alexander's army would actually come across.

Then Alexander used the same trick at night. He built bonfires, marched his men to the edge of the river, and ordered them to yell war cries and blow their trumpets. Again, Porus scrambled to meet the challenge that never came. His army and elephants lay in wait all night in the soaking rains while Alexander and his men got a good night's sleep.

Alexander kept the fake attacks going for two weeks during the torrential rains. Porus's army seethed with anger and irritation. But, really, what else could they do?

▲ Stampeding war elephant

Meanwhile, Alexander's scouts found a wooded area upstream where they could cross unseen. To keep the enemy off the scent, Alexander left a "stunt double"—dressed in his armor—and a decoy force at the fake crossing site. Then, with mud sucking at their feet and water up to their armpits, Alexander and his army sneaked across the swollen Hydaspes River. By the time Porus got a clue, it was too late. Alexander's army was across—and ready to get their game on.

But there was one small problem: Nobody knew how to fight the elephants.

LIKE TANKS WITH TRUNKS

Most of Alexander's men had never even seen elephants before. And they just about wet their loincloths when they spied Porus's line of two hundred trained war elephants. The Greeks' own horses stood only about five-and-half-feet tall. How would they fight hundreds of tusked, twelve-foot monsters? Suddenly their spears and swords looked about as powerful as toothpicks. Was Alexander's awesome army about to be destroyed by Dumbo's ancestors?

But Alexander had a plan. He spread out his forces to en-circle the enemy. Then he gave two orders: to wipe out the elephant handlers and to harass—but not kill—the elephants that were trapped in the center. Why save the elephants? Alexander had learned from local elephant handlers that injured elephants don't run. They stampede. They create chaos and confusion. And they can't tell the difference between a Greek and an Indian warrior. When Alexander trapped most of the Indian army in the center, Porus's own men were the ones who got stomped flatter than gum on a sidewalk.

▲ Greeks' horses stood only about five-and-half-feet tall.

Once again, Alexander turned the enemy's strongest weapon into their worse nightmare. King Porus had no choice but to call it quits.

"WE ARE SO DONE!"

Soon after the victory over Porus in India, Alexander's own men waved the white flag. Their outcry was loud and clear: *No more! We insist on going home.* Alexander was stunned. They'd only just gotten started! He tried talking his officers out of giving up.

"You owe it to yourselves to leave nothing untried, nothing passed by because of fear," he implored them. He urged them to keep going just because they *could*. He promised to lay the world's riches at their feet. But his men only stared at him, unmoved.

He tried guilt: "I who ask you [to continue our campaign in India] have never given you a command without first exposing myself to the risks involved, and I have often protected your line with my own shield."

Again, silence.

"I must have done you some wrong without knowing it," exclaimed Alexander, growing angrier, "because you do not even want to look at me."

Finally, one officer spoke up in a daring "let my people go" speech. "Do not try to lead men who are unwilling to follow you," he begged, reminding Alexander that his men hadn't been home in almost ten years. "Every [one of us] longs to see our parents again . . . or our wives and children. Sir, if there is one thing above all others a successful man should know, it is *when to stop.*"

At that, Alexander's officers didn't cheer—they wept.

Alexander flew into a rage. He threatened to find other fighters who wouldn't "desert" their king. Then he stomped off and refused to talk to anybody for two days. On the third day, Alexander asked his seers to read the omens to see what would happen if he continued his campaign. Their answer? You might as well forget about it.

Alexander had to face the cold, hard truth—he had lost his first battle. He couldn't talk his men into following him into the rest of India, so he reluctantly agreed to turn back, although promising to return with "fresh" soldiers who were not afraid to fight for him.

He never guessed that he'd lose that battle, too.

ANCIENT WARFARE:
ALEXANDER'S BAG OF TRICKS

Alexander's genius for trickery in battle went beyond the "fake attack" scam he used against King Porus of India. Here are a few others from his bag of tricks:

- **The "Sneak Up from Behind" Trap.** One of Alexander's standard ploys, he used this trap when an enemy blocked a mountain pass. Alexander sent his men to secretly cut steps into the side of a mountain away from his opponent's view. He left a decoy army at the pass and sneaked his powerful fighters around the back of the mountain in preparation for an ambush. Before the enemy knew it, Alexander's army was at their rear. Stunned, their foes always surrendered without a fight.

- **The "Scare 'Em Silly" Ploy.** During a march through a mountain pass, a band of barbarians trapped Alexander's men between a river and some hills. Outnumbered and surrounded, Alexander commanded his men to perform their standard military drills in total silence. Mesmerized by the strange "dance," the barbarians crept closer to watch. Then Alexander gave the order for his men to beat on their shields and scream bloody murder. In the echoing valley, the commotion probably sounded like all the ghouls of the underworld had escaped at once. The barbarians panicked and hightailed it out of there, scrambling over each other to escape. Then Alexander and his men sauntered untouched through the pass.

- **The "Up All Night" Trick.** Alexander used this one on both King Darius in Persia and King Porus in India. He pretended that he was going to attack at night (or leaked word he "might" attack during the night), forcing his enemy to stay awake just in case. Then he got a good night's sleep and attacked for real in the morning—easily whipping a bleary-eyed enemy.

- **The "Make 'Em Think You're Giants" Ruse.** When Alexander left India, he didn't want the people he had just conquered to think they could take back what he had just claimed. So he came up with a plan to keep them scared 24/7. He ordered his men to build a camp filled with giant wooden beds, tables, and chairs. This way, anybody who happened upon the camp would think his men were giants—and wouldn't *dare* attack.

"GREAT" MINDS THINK ALIKE...

Great leaders from Julius Caesar to Napoleon admired Alexander's genius for trickery. They even sounded like Alexander!

I came, I saw, I conquered.
—JULIUS CAESAR

Victory belongs to the most persevering.
—NAPOLEON BONAPARTE

Ω

CHAPTER 9

THE BEGINNING OF THE END

*Those who aim at great deeds
must also suffer greatly.*

—PLUTARCH

∏

To Alexander, his men's refusal to march on was a monumental defeat. After all, he stood on the edge of conquering all of ancient India. What a time for his men to get homesick on him! Now he had to turn around and take them back to Greece. Frustrated? Worse than a Super Bowl quarterback discovering his team left the field at halftime. To watch figure skating. And eat bon-bons. In fluffy slippers.

But Alexander got his revenge—he marched his men the "long way" home. Ever the sensible conqueror, he figured he could sack more cities and grab even more territory along the way. But what seemed like a practical idea to Alexander practically cost him his life.

He hugged the coast near the Gulf of Oman and ordered the men to sack every city they found. Attacking defenseless cities and folding them into the kingdom was the kind of thing his men could do in their sleep. Imagine their surprise when they found themselves toe-to-toe with a group of fierce fighters—the Mallians—who preferred to die rather than lose their independence.

Faster than his men could say, "There's no place like home," Alexander's detour turned into a rugged tour of duty.

MAULED BY THE MALLIANS

After several bloody skirmishes with Alexander's army, the Mallians barricaded themselves behind a fortress. Alexander called for ladders to scale the enemy's walls. But his men moved too slowly for the impatient Alexander. He snatched a ladder from the poor guy who was carrying it, threw it against the fortress, and scrambled up to the top.

Shocked, his men could only stare as their king took on the Mallian defenders atop the wall. A handful of them rushed at Alexander, but he cut them down with his sword. In his shining armor, the king quickly became a target for everything the enemy could throw at him: spears, arrows, javelins, and rocks.

Alexander's men panicked for his safety. They scrambled for more ladders, clawing at each other to climb up

▲ The ladder breaks as Alexander and his men scale the Mallian Wall.

first. But so many men tried to go up at the same time that the ladders began to shred under their weight. Only three men made it to the top before the ladders completely collapsed.

The king faced an entire enemy army virtually alone.

Going for the Glory

Alexander suddenly realized his vulnerability. On one side stood countless enemy fighters ready to tear him apart. On the other was the safety of his own troops. A more cautious man would have jumped back into the protection of his men. But "cautious" was not in Alexander's vocabulary. He leapt straight into the enemy's compound.

More Mallians sprang at him, but he easily cut them down, too. Afraid to challenge him with the sword, the enemy formed a half-circle around Alexander and hurled everything they could find at him.

The three men who had made it over the wall with Alexander jumped in to help their king. One took a spear in the face and died instantly, but the other two fought on either side of their king.

Meanwhile, his panicked men on the other side of the wall scraped, crawled, and crashed their way into the place just in time to see Alexander take a hit. An arrow pierced his armor and sliced into his lung. Air and blood gushed from the wound. Alexander continued to fight until he collapsed onto his shield.

A cry of grief and rage rose from every warrior when they saw their downed king. They were on the enemy in an instant, slaughtering the Mallians and rushing the king to safety.

Rumors spread that Alexander had been killed, and his men wept openly. Who would lead them now? How would they get home? The warlike tribes surrounding them would surely attack once the "the dread of Alexander's name was a thing of the past."

But they panicked too early. Alexander may have been down, but he wasn't out.

It's All Greek to Me!

Ω

You will never do anything in this world without courage. It is the greatest quality of the mind next to honor.

—ARISTOTLE

Cut It Out. *I Mean It.*

Soldiers carried the semi-conscious Alexander back to his tent. Alexander's doctor turned pale when he saw the wound. One false move and they would both die—the king from his injury and the doctor for failing to save him.

Alexander looked at the doctor and rasped, "Why are you waiting? If I have to die, why do you not at least free me from this agony as soon as possible?" The doctor signaled for his men to hold the king down as he prepared to cut the arrowhead out of his lung, but Alexander waved them off. He "had no need of people to hold him," he claimed. He could handle it without flinching. When the doctor cut into his flesh, so much blood poured out that Alexander fainted. His friends in the tent wailed, thinking he had died.

But against the odds—lung surgery with no anesthesia, no sterilized instruments, and no antibiotics—the king recovered. No wonder people thought he was part god. That he survived the attack was amazing; that he lived through the surgery was miraculous.

Unfortunately, he was going to need more than a miracle to survive his next challenge.

Nightmare in the Desert

Within months of his near-death experience, a recovering Alexander continued his march along the Indian coast. His navy kept pace, supplying the ground troops with food and water.

But just as they approached the Gedrosian Desert (near Baluchistan in modern Pakistan), Alexander lost contact with his ships. The army—as many as fifty thousand men, along with thousands of pack animals and countless women and children—faced a long march through the desert without back-up food or water.

▲ Alexander and his men cross the Gedrosian Desert.

Thousands dropped and died of thirst and heat exhaustion. Not fully healed from his lung injury, Alexander must have been in agony from the searing heat. At one point, his men found a small puddle of water, scooped it up in a helmet, and brought it to Alexander. But he wouldn't touch it. If his men couldn't drink, he wouldn't drink. He poured it out. Everybody was amazed and heartened by this act. It was "as good as a drink for every man in the army," claimed one ancient historian.

Alexander and his ships eventually reconnected. The fiasco made everyone wonder if Alexander had lost his golden touch. But his next move made everyone wonder if he'd lost his mind.

AN OUTRAGEOUS SCHEME

During the long trek back to Greece (by way of Persia), Alexander continued to wonder how he could create harmony and unity among the races in his multicultural empire. So he came up with an outrageous scheme: forced intermarriage. If the Greeks and Persians married, he figured, maybe they'd learn to love each other and live peacefully together.

In the Persian city of Susa, Alexander commanded ninety-two of his officers to marry Persian noblewomen during a mass ceremony. He paid his men handsomely with hefty dowries, or bride payments, out of his own pocket. He even took a second wife, the daughter of King Darius. (We can only imagine that Roxane, back in the palace at Babylon, wasn't too happy about this.) To the ten thousand other Greeks who had married locals during the past ten years away from home, Alexander sent wedding

▲ The mass weddings at Susa

gifts. "My intention by [these] sacred union[s]," Alexander explained, was to "erase all distinction between conquered and conqueror."

But it backfired. Already seething at the way Alexander had adopted Persian customs, his men resented being forced to marry Persian women. How dare he meddle in their private lives!

Alexander was about to learn a painful lesson: You can't force people to love each other. But you can get them to hate you if you try.

MUTINY AT OPIS

In the Persian city of Opis, Alexander announced his older and injured warriors could finally go home. And, as a parting gift, he was sending them off with enough money to make their neighbors jealous.

He expected cheers and applause. Instead he got mutiny. The assembly erupted in anger. The men shouted that "every man in the army" should be discharged, not only the old and injured. They told Alexander he "could take his father with him" (meaning Zeus) on his next campaign.

Homesick after so many years, exhausted by endless marches, and angry with Alexander for replacing old Greek soldiers with young Persian men all the way up the ranks to the sacred Companion cavalry, the army had finally had it. They hated how he had made his officers marry Persian women. And they detested all the ways

▲ Alexander puts down the mutiny at Opis.

he'd "gone Persian"—from the bowing to the adoption of Persian clothing.

Somehow Alexander didn't see this coming. He roared out a tirade and reminded the men that when they'd first set out, most of them were so poor they "wore skins." He stated that—thanks to him—they now had more wealth than they could have ever imagined. And, he continued, he had suffered right along with them.

"Does any man among you honestly feel that he has suffered more for me than I have suffered for him? There is no part of my body . . . which has not a scar; not a weapon a man may grasp or fling the mark of which I do not carry upon me."

"Some of you have owed money," he went on. "And I have paid your debts, never troubling to inquire how they were incurred, and in spite of the fact that you earn good pay and grow rich from the sack of cities."

Disgusted, he waved them away. "Out of my sight!" he bellowed. He stomped off to his room and refused to see anybody for two days. On the third day he sent for his Persian officers and divided the command of his entire army between them.

The Greeks were stunned. Alexander had called their bluff. He replaced every single one of them with a Persian.

WE DIDN'T MEAN IT—REALLY!

The Greek officers rushed to Alexander's quarters and begged his forgiveness.

They wept.

They wailed.

They groveled.

The groveling worked.

When a tearful Alexander emerged, a Companion cavalry officer cried, "My lord, what hurts us is that you have made Persians your kinsmen [and not us]." There it was again: jealousy.

But "every man of you I regard as my kinsman," Alexander exclaimed in reconciliation. "And from now on that is what I shall call you."

▲ Persian magi

That night he hosted a huge banquet—a party for both Persians and Greeks. Greek seers and Persian magi led the prayers together. And Alexander himself prayed "that Persians and Macedonians might rule together in harmony."

It was a great dream. Too bad it never came true.

DEATH COMES CALLING

Three months after the reconciliation banquet, Alexander's best friend since boyhood—Hephaestion—died. Some blame disease; others, poison. Either way, Alexander was devastated.

He fasted and secluded himself for two days after Hephaestion's death. Some say the king never got over the loss of the one friend he could always count on. Alexander buried his grief by planning more adventures and conquests. But within seven months of Hephaestion's death, Alexander also became gravely ill.

In Babylon, Alexander struggled with fever for nine days before he called his top officers to his bedside. He took off his ring and handed it to one of his generals. Alexander's friends, realizing this was the end, asked, "To whom do you leave the kingdom?" With his last breath, he whispered, "To the strongest," a line from *The Iliad*.

And then the self-proclaimed son of Zeus did something nobody thought he'd ever do. He died.

▲ Alexander's funeral procession

WHAT KILLED HIM?

Alexander of Macedon was dead at thirty-two. Within five years of his death, rumors swirled that he'd been poisoned. Most modern historians are split between poison and malaria as the cause of death. Some current scholars also claim he died of liver disease from drinking too much wine. We'll never know for sure.

We do know this: The unity Alexander tried to create blew apart. Virtually all of his officers renounced the Persian wives they had been forced to marry. Then they turned on each other. Each of Alexander's generals claimed he was the "strongest"—and tried to prove it

▲ A bust of Ptolemy

on the battlefield. Friends fought friends in a massive land grab that carved up the kingdom.

In fact, Greek generals fought over Alexander's lands for forty years in what's called the "Wars of the Successors." By the time the dust cleared, three top guys had taken over: Antigonus in Greece; Seleucus in Syria, Babylon, and Turkey; and Ptolemy in Egypt. And not one of them gave a hoot about native customs or integrating locals into power. In fact, each of the "successors" installed a pure Greek rule in his kingdom.

Alexander's dream of unity died with him.

▲ Coins depicting Antigonus

▲ Coins depicting Seleucus

ANCIENT MYSTERIES:
THE INVASION OF THE BODY SNATCHER

Alexander's mummified body was on its way back to Greece when Ptolemy snatched it. He took it with him to Egypt and named himself pharaoh.

So you could say that Ptolemy stole Egypt over Alexander's dead body.

Ptolemy put Alexander's body in a golden casket and showed him off in a mausoleum in Alexandria. Alexander's body became a huge tourist attraction. Over the years, people began stealing from his burial chamber. The biggest thieves were Roman emperors, who eventually took over all of Alexander's kingdoms. Augustus and Caligula reportedly stole Alexander's cloak, ring, breastplate, and shield. They believed that if they owned the great king's possessions, they might own his power and brilliance, too.

▲ Augustus

▲ Caligula

▲ Alexander's sarcophagus? Most scholars believe it belongs to someone else, even though its engravings depict Alexander.

Fat chance.

Eventually Alexander's tomb disappeared completely. But many believe it still may lay somewhere deep beneath the streets of modern Alexandria, just waiting to be found.

CHAPTER 10

HERO—OR MONSTER?

Dignity does not consist in possessing honors,
but in deserving them.

—ARISTOTLE

W hat a guy. More than twenty-three hundred years after his death, people still argue about Alexander. On one side you have hero-worshippers, the ones who glory in his victories and breakthroughs. They believe Alexander's legacy was to leave the world a better place.

On the other you have Alex-bashers, people who think his warmongering made him worse than the devil himself. To them, Alexander joined a cast of power-hungry characters who have dotted history with bloodshed and suffering.

So who's right? Was he a hero or a monster?

Or was he a little bit of both?

ON THE HERO SIDE: ALEXANDER THE *GR-R-R-REAT*

Hero-worshippers point to Alexander's brilliance on the battlefield and his undefeated record. They emphasize that he was the first to open the East to the West. They marvel at the way he unified nations through trade and culture. And they admire Alexander's vision of a unified world, his uncommon respect for women, and his commitment to religious tolerance. Most importantly, they believe that Alexander saved democracy by spreading its ideals (if not its practice) around the world.

So, for some people calling the young king "Alexander the Great" makes sense.

▲ A bust of Alexander the Great

A LEGEND BY ANY OTHER NAME

Throughout the ages, most people have considered Alexander a hero. Even today, Greek fishermen call on Alexander to calm stormy seas. Leaders from modern Greece and Macedonia (formerly Yugoslavia) have nearly come to blows in a fight to claim Alexander as their own son. In Pakistan, storytellers gather children by the campfire to tell stories of *Sikander e Aazem*. And in Afghanistan, legend has it that some tribal leaders, well into the 1950s, fought under the ancient flag of Alexander, a relic of the days when they were unified under the young king.

▲ Greek fishermen

READ ALL ABOUT IT!
ALEXANDER LAUNCHES THE HELLENISTIC AGE!

Historians mark the Hellenistic Age as the time between Alexander's death in 323 BCE and the takeover of Greece by the Romans in 146 BCE. Hellenism (from the word *Hellene*, translated as "Greek") came to mean "imitating the Greeks." Today most of the modern world has imitated American music and popular culture by listening to rock-and-roll, drinking soda, and wearing blue jeans. Likewise, the ancient world copied Greek culture: they learned and spoke Greek, studied Plato, and wore tunics.

Alexander was the Johnny Appleseed of the ancient world. Only instead of dropping apple seeds, he sprinkled Greek soldiers, engineers, architects, artists, and settlers in every city he conquered. Thanks to Alexander, these cities sprouted Greek gymnasiums, temples with Corinthian columns, classical sculptures, and theaters featuring Greek plays. Greek became the common language of politics, business, and education. Wherever people went, they had to speak Alexander's native tongue. No Greek, no speak. And fashion-wise, the "Greek look" was so common that even Buddhist monks in ancient India copied it. That's why many of the statues of the Buddha show him wearing Greek tunics rather than native Indian clothing.

Which just goes to show that even in the ancient world, *chic* happens.

Alexander also founded as many as seventy cities, naming most of them after himself, of course. In fact, Alexander's pet city, Alexandria in Egypt, became the shining example of a new international Hellenized city. It served as the business and cultural center of the era. Just like Alexandria, all of his cities were modeled after Greek cities back home—from the grid of the streets to the placement of the temples. In fact, many of the cities Alexander conquered and built didn't just look Greek—they acted Greek, too. They had "nearly" democratic governments in which citizens had the right to vote, but with one catch: They had to pledge allegiance to the king first.

Funny, isn't it? The son of the king who destroyed democracy in Greece was the same man who brought its ideals to the rest of the world.

ANCIENT LEGENDS:
CLEOPATRA'S LONG LOST UNCLE?

The coolest queen to come out of the ancient world could have been Alexander's long-lost niece. Really. Here's how: When Alexander died, his good friend Ptolemy took Egypt and became a powerful pharaoh. Ptolemy grew up with Alexander and fought beside him in most battles. He kept a diary of Alexander's adventures, which is how most of the stories about the young king were preserved. Ptolemy claimed that Philip was his father, making him Alexander's half-brother. This could have been true, although nobody knows for sure. Either way, Ptolemy's descendants ruled for hundreds of years, ending with a certain beautiful queen: Cleopatra, the last of the Ptolemies. If the elder Ptolemy's

▲ Cleopatra VII, the last of the Ptolemy rulers

claim to Alexander's bloodline was true, then Alexander was also Cleopatra's long-(*long!*) lost uncle. Or half-uncle, at least.

Under the rule of the Ptolemies, Egypt thrived—until the Romans came knocking. Julius Caesar wanted Egypt under his rule, but the brilliant queen Cleopatra had other plans. She made a deal with Caesar's general, Marc Antony: If he helped her defeat the Romans, he could rule Egypt with her. But Roman forces easily defeated Antony and Cleopatra's navy. When Cleopatra heard that her armies had been defeated, she did what any Homeric hero would do—she killed herself.

Alexander would've understood: Death was preferable to defeat.

When Cleopatra died, she took the last gasps of Hellenism with her. The Age of the Romans began.

FRIEND OF THE FAITHFUL

It's also ironic that the man known for conquering the world through war is the same man who introduced the concept of peace through religious tolerance. Of course, Alexander never used the words "religious tolerance." Respecting others people's religion was just something he did, inspired by his own faith. Until the day he died, Alexander led morning prayers and rituals, just as his mother had taught him (without the snakes, though).

Even as he sacked Persian and Indian cities, Alexander respected and protected their religious leaders. He brought Persian magi, Egyptian priests, and Indian holy men into his inner circle—which also included Greek seers—and often strengthened the native religious ruling classes. But Alexander's heart wasn't all incense and flowers. He also knew that foreign rulers who removed priests and religious leaders eventually faced rebellions and murder attempts from angry believers. By giving control back to the religious classes, Alexander earned their undying trust and loyalty—and their taxes.

Today all of the world's major religions acknowledge Alexander in some way. Judaism honors him as an enlightened king who respected their faith. Mainstream Islam names him as a prophet who unified the Middle East, preparing the Arab world to receive Mohammed. Many Hindus believe that Alexander was the model for Skanda, the God of War. And some Christians believe that by making Greek the universal language, Alexander paved the way for Christianity to spread throughout the ancient world.

▲ Alexander practicing religious tolerance

▲ Middle Eastern priests

ANCIENT RELIGIONS:
MYSTIC MELTING POT

IN INDIA

Alexander's interest in other faiths went deep. In India, Alexander met the "Naked Philosophers"—priests who gave up everything (okay, so they weren't *actually* naked) to focus on the inner life. Alexander approached one priest, Calanus, to ask him questions about his faith. Angry at having his country invaded, the holy man refused to talk to Alexander. He didn't care who Alexander was. He wouldn't talk to him even "if the Greek came from Zeus himself."

For a man with nothing, the priest had a lot of gall.

Any other king would have had the holy man jailed for disrespect—at the very least. But Alexander admired courage—and his interest in the man's faith kept him pursuing the Indian priest. Eventually the two became fast friends. Calanus even left his band of Naked Philosophers to join Alexander on the king's journey home.

Wherever he went, Alexander's genuine interest and openness to other faiths opened doors and softened hearts.

IN JERUSALEM

Just how deep did Alexander's religious respect go? According to a story handed down by Jewish lore, when he was on his way to Egypt, Alexander stopped in Jerusalem. The Hebrew archpriest, Simon the Just, met him at the gates of the city. Instead of waiting for the archpriest to come to him—the typical royal protocol—Alexander jumped off his horse and walked to Simon. Alexander's top general had a fit. How dare Alexander walk toward the priest! Didn't he know the archpriest should've come to *him*?

Alexander's response? "I did not greet the archpriest, but the *god* he represents."

Modern scholars claim that there's no proof this ever happened, but Jewish people continue to honor Alexander as one of the few ancient leaders who respected their religion. The young king's appreciation for other faiths has earned him the loyalty of religious leaders the world over.

THE "GREAT" LEGACIES

In the wake of Alexander's influence, a Middle Eastern renaissance began. Scientists and mathematicians in Egypt, Turkey, and Iran made huge discoveries. Euclid invented geometry; Archimedes identified key mathematical laws of physics and became the father of integral calculus; and Aristarchus of Samos discovered that the earth revolved around the sun (rather than the other way around, which Westerners believed until the 1600s). One scientist in Egypt even came up with nearly accurate measurements for the circumference of the earth.

Under Hellenism, a radical idea began to grow—that education was for the poor as well as the rich, for girls as well as boys. In some cities in Persia and Egypt, rich and poor children alike learned reading, writing, and arithmetic.

Thanks in part to greater educational opportunities, women began to catch a break, even moving into male-dominated fields such as medicine. For example, Hagnodice trained in Alexandria in 300 BCE and became the first woman doctor. Women lectured as philosophers, wrote poetry, and painted. They participated in civic life and, in some cities, owned property and served as magistrates, or judges. Women even ruled as powerful queens in Egypt. It's sad but true: many women in the Hellenized Middle East had more freedom and opportunity than women in the same countries today.

Alexander's co-mingling of Greek and Persian cultures kept the Middle East (Egypt, Turkey, Iran, and Iraq) thriving economically and intellectually for hundreds of years after his death. In fact, such enormous strides were made that historians divide ancient history into "Before Alexander" and "After Alexander."

Good or bad, that's one monster of a legacy.

IT'S ALL GRΣΣK TO MΣ!

Ω

[Alexander] had great personal beauty, invincible power of endurance, and a keen intellect; he was brave and adventurous, strict in the observance of his religious duties, and hungry for fame. . . . Never in the world was there another like him.

—ARRIAN

ANCIENT FAMILIES:
WHAT HAPPENED TO THE WOMEN IN ALEXANDER'S LIFE?

Being a woman in the ancient world was tough enough, but it was murder if you were related to Alexander. Almost all of the women in Alexander's life came to an untimely end.

The Mother of All Furies. Olympias, Alexander's mother, was like a Category Four Hurricane—all wind and fury and lashing attacks. And her personality didn't change after Alexander's death. Olympias reportedly made a play at ruling Greece, but lost. Antigonus, the new ruler, kept her isolated for years. He probably wanted her dead, but nobody dared touch the mother of the great Alexander. Eventually she was murdered by the relatives of the people she had murdered. (Remember the young bride and baby she was said to have eliminated?)

Lovely Wife, Brutal Widow. Alexander's first wife, Roxane, was pregnant when Alexander died. A few months later, she gave birth to a boy, Alexander IV, the only true heir. The beautiful Roxane was a lot like Alexander's mother. When her husband died, she quickly called his other Persian wife to her side—not to cry on her shoulder,

▲ Roxane holding her son, Alexander IV

but to kill her. Like Olympias, she didn't want any other competitors for the throne. Unfortunately, when young Alexander was twelve, both mother and son were murdered.

▲ The family of Darius III before Alexander

Persia's Queen Mother. The mother of Alexander's archenemy eventually became one of his closest friends, which is pretty amazing if you think about it. Queen Sisygambis was the mother of the defeated Darius and grandmother of Alexander's second Persian wife—the one he married in the mass ceremony. Queen Sisygambis and Alexander stayed close until his death. He respected her wisdom and experience. She probably schooled him on Persian customs. When Sisygambis learned that Alexander had died and that Roxane had killed her grand-daughter, Alexander's second wife, she turned her face to the wall and refused to eat or drink—an ancient form of suicide.

▲ Queen Sisygambis bows to Alexander.

Baby Sister, Future Queen. Alexander's father and mother had another child after Alexander—a daughter named Cleopatra (a common Greek name that would later belong to the famous Egyptian queen). We know very little about Alexander's sister, except that her father married her off to her uncle, the king of a different kingdom, to keep the peace. Did Alexander's little sister look like him? Was she as intense? As driven? As brilliant? Sadly we'll never know.

ON THE MONSTER SIDE: ALEXANDER THE GREEDY

Of course, not everyone thinks Alexander was so "great." The Alex-bashers point out that Alexander invaded other people's lands, stole their wealth, and slaughtered countless innocent people. They claim that he was a heavy-drinking egomaniac who stopped at nothing in his obsession to rule the world. They consider him the poster child for unchecked power. And they question his sanity—especially after he began to believe in his own divinity.

Finally, they point out that Alexander, together with his father, killed democracy in Athens when they put all of Greece under a king's rule.

THE NO-SO-GREAT LEGACIES

Alexander's ideals of tolerance, equality, and unity were breakthrough concepts. Too bad some of his other legacies weren't as noble. The worst? His belief that war was a noble path to personal glory.

Of course, Alexander didn't invent the idea that war equaled glory. Mankind had been warring with each other since the dawn of time. It's just that Alexander made war seem so darn heroic. But the ugly truth of war is that countless innocent people get killed or displaced. There's nothing heroic about that.

Not surprisingly, Alexander's amazing victories also transformed warfare and the military. Warfare became more strategic and small forces (like his cavalry) become more specialized. And just about every nation in the world adopted the idea of having a full-time army, a concept that Philip introduced and Alexander perfected.

Military leaders throughout the ages—from Julius Caesar to Napoleon Bonaparte—have tried to copy Alexander's model of world domination through military conquest. Few have ever matched his brilliance on the battlefield.

Sadly, for the millions killed in their efforts, that never stopped them from trying.

Despite Alexander's "religious tolerance," at least one faith doesn't think Alexander was so "enlightened." Today's Zoroastrians—the last surviving followers of King Darius's ancient religion in Iran—call him "Alexander the Accursed." Why? Because he defeated their ancient king and destroyed their sacred texts in a palace fire.

Alexander may have defeated their king, but the truth is he never attacked their religion. Like

▲ Modern-day Zoroastrians honor fire during an annual ceremony.

many pagan religions of the period, they were swallowed up by the rise of Islam and the Ottoman Empire hundreds of years after Alexander.

BUT IN THE END . . .

Whatever people believe about Alexander, there's no denying that the man transformed the world. Good or bad, he created something never seen before or since: a world unified by one king, one language, one currency, and one amazing experiment in religious tolerance and racial diversity.

Alexander of Macedon . . .
  started out as a teen . . .
    became a warrior . . .
      morphed into a war hero . . .
        and died king of the world.

Ω

Chapter Endnotes and Quote Attributions

Ω

Of the ancient historians, only Plutarch wrote about Alexander's youth. Diodorus, Arrian, and Rufus began recording his story when Alexander took the throne at the age of twenty, and they focused primarily on his military conquests.

CHAPTER 1: A Wild and Crazy Family

1. Page 11: Plutarch was one of the last of the classical Greek historians; he wrote in 66 ACE. In *Age of Alexander*, he wrote that on the day of Alexander's birth, Philip also captured a barbarian city, his general captured another city in a great battle, and his racehorse won a victory at the Olympic Games. The soothsayers claimed that all these victories meant his son would prove to be "invincible." (Plutarch 254)
2. Page 16: Plutarch claimed that Alexander wanted the glory, not the riches, of being a king.

CHAPTER 2: Greek Boy Wonder

1. Page 19: The Persians were convinced that Philip's "astuteness" was nothing compared to his son's spirit. (Plutarch 256)
2. Page 21: Alexander's horse, Bucephalas, cost thirteen talents. One talent, some scholars say, was probably the equivalent of an ounce or so of gold. (Plutarch 257)
3. Page 22: Philip wasn't the only one moved by Alexander's success with the horse; the "rest of the company broke into loud applause" as Alexander cantered the horse back. (Plutarch 258)
4. Page 26: Plutarch claims that Alexander "disproved of the whole race of trained athletes." We can only presume that he thought of trained athletes as being vain, but trained warriors as being heroic. (Plutarch 256)

CHAPTER 3: School of Hard Knocks

1. Page 31: Alexander shared Leonidas's "training" habits with Queen Ada of Persia. The older Queen tried to ply Alexander with sweets when he visited, but he always refused. Concerned about his "temperate" eating, she even offered him bakers and cooks. That's when he explained that Leonidas had trained him to eat sparingly. (Plutarch 277)
2. Page 32: Some modern historians claim that this just proves Alexander could hold a grudge for a really, really long time. (Plutarch 281; Peter Green, *Alexander of Macedon: A Historical Biography*. Conjecture on the worth of the spices also by Green.)
3. Page 33: Philip learned early what all parents of smart, strong-willed children eventually learn: appealing to his intellect and being persuasive worked better than barking orders. (Plutarch 258)
4. Page 34: Diodorus was a Greek/Italian historian who wrote between 80–20 BCE. The friend Alexander saved from the poisoned arrow was none other than Ptolemy, the man who would take over Egypt after Alexander's death and whose line would rule Egypt for centuries. (Diodorus Siculus, *Library of History Books XVI.66–XVII*, 417)
5. Page 37: Plutarch claimed that Alexander "never lost the devotion to philosophy" that Aristotle inspired. (Plutarch 260)

CHAPTER 4: Teenage Grecian Heroic Warrior

1. Page 41: Diodorus claimed that Alexander had his "heart set" on showing his father his "prowess" on the battlefield. (Diodorus page 79)
2. Page 47: Alexander's Macedonian advisors underestimated his determination to pursue his father's plans for Persia. They also learned that as soon as people told Alexander he "couldn't do something," he'd go all out to prove them wrong. (Plutarch 263)
3. Page 49: Arrian was a Greek-born Roman soldier and military historian who wrote in 90 ACE. Many Thebans were "anxious to approach Alexander" and ask forgiveness for the revolt. Alexander had a history of forgiving "traitors" as long as they recommitted to him. Who knows what might have happened if the majority of soldiers who didn't want to fight had prevailed? Instead, to prove a point, Alexander razed the city; thousands were killed, and countless women and children were sold into captivity. Nobody dared question Alexander's rule after that. (Arrian, *The Campaigns of Alexander*, 57)

CHAPTER 5: "Ready or Not, Here I Come!"

1. Page 52: Like many great leaders, Alexander always had a flair for the dramatic. (Diodorus 163)
2. Page 52: The general in question was Parmenio, Philip's right-hand man and a brilliant commander in his own right. (Arrian 70)
3. Page 53: Quintus Curtius Rufus was a Roman soldier and historian who wrote in 41 ACE. He cites how Alexander's stubbornness would not let him admit the risk of crossing the River Granicus after a full day of marching. (Rufus, *The History of Alexander* 23)
4. Page 54: Before the Persians fell, those fighting closest to Alexander "went all out to slay the king." Despite the fearsome attacks, Alexander persevered. (Diodorus 175)
5. Page 55: Alexander had a gift for making his soldiers feel and act more heroic. (Arrian 76)
6. Page 57: Despite Alexander's unorthodox solution, the consensus of the witnesses was that the prophecy of the Gordian Knot would be fulfilled. (Arrian 105)
7. Pages 58-59: As Darius sneaked up behind Alexander's forces, he came upon a hospital filled with Alexander's injured and sick soldiers. He had them all butchered in their beds. (Arrian 111) Alexander never repaid the atrocity in kind. (Renault, *The Nature of Alexander*, 92)
8. Page 59: Alexander continued to pump up his men by telling them they "shall fight for Greece—and our hearts will be in it." Meanwhile, many of the Persian mercenaries fought only for money. (Arrian 112)
9. Page 60: Alexander was "firm in his refusal to suspect treachery in friends." (Arrian 107)
10. Page 60: Alexander used "Mother" as a term of friendly respect. Alexander promised to keep her safe, and he restored her wealth and dignity. Queen Sisygambis, along with her daughters, wept, "so great was their unexpected joy" at Alexander's kind treatment of them. Over time, she did, indeed, see him as a second son. (Diodorus 225)
11. Page 60: The woman in question was a freeborn Greek courtesan (the only class of women with any sort of freedom); even so, Alexander encouraged him to win her by love and not by other means. (Plutarch 299)
12. Page 61: The wealth of the Persians would continue to astonish Alexander throughout his campaign. (Plutarch 275)
13. Page 62: The woman's fearlessness in facing Alexander—her "dignity of spirit" despite her losses—impressed him. Alexander admired courage in whatever form it took. (Plutarch 265)

CHAPTER 6: Egypt and the Final Face-Off

1. Page 66: Plutarch says that Alexander adopted a "haughty and majestic bearing" toward Persians/Egyptians because they had a tradition of believing their kings were divine; however, he was more relaxed with the Greeks. (Plutarch 284)
2. Page 67: The Egyptian priest predicted that Alexander "would be unconquerable for all time." (Diodorus 267)
3. Pages 68-69: Alexander's restless genius resulted in a city that eventually replaced Athens as the center of the commercial and intellectual world. Alexandria was a key seaport, serving as the central point of trade between the East and West. The famous library at Alexandria attracted scholars the world over. The city even featured a science museum that was a top tourist attraction. (Arrian 149)
4. Page 70: Arrian claims that it wasn't out of "vanity" that Alexander refused to fight, but that it made "perfectly sound sense" because night fighting is "tricky business." (Arrian 163)
5. Page 70: The brooding "hour after hour" over an attack that never came wore the Persians down. (Arrian 164)
6. Page 71: Alexander displayed this bigger-than-life and "steadfast confidence" throughout all the fighting, too. (Plutarch 289)
7. Page 73: Arrian states that Alexander instructed the people to restore their ancient temple, but he doesn't describe their reaction. We can only assume that they were very grateful. (Arrian 173)
8. Page 73: Alexander placed the Persian commander, Mazaeus, in charge as Governor of Babylon. If he felt that locals were loyal, he frequently put them in charge of their own cities. (Rufus 96)
9. Page 75: Alexander would not board the boat to Persia until he had "assigned an estate, a village to another or the revenues" to soldiers who were struggling financially. (Plutarch 267)
10. Page 75: Alexander was so generous that he was "always more offended with those who refused his gifts than with those who asked for them." (Plutarch 296)
11. Page 75: By being so generous to the families of the fallen, Alexander earned the undying loyalty from present and future citizens. (Arrian 75)

CHAPTER 7: Can't We All Just Get Along?

1. Page 79: Alexander drew the line at "outlandish" clothing such as trousers (!) and refused to wear the Persian tiara. (Plutarch 301 and 302)
2. Page 79: At first, the Macedonians conceded that Alexander could dress as a Persian leader because they knew that adopting Persian dress would increase his prestige in public. (Plutarch 302)
3. Page 80: Training thirty thousand young Persian boys to integrate the officer class of a unified army was a move ahead of its time. Still, his men hated the idea. (Arrian 356)
4. Page 81: Their first mistake was telling Alexander that he couldn't get his men up the rock. (Arrian 233)
5. Page 81: Later, the leader praised Alexander's "sense of honor and justice," presumably because Alexander didn't kill him. (Arrian 237)
6. Page 82: Plutarch says that Alexander's marriage to Roxane was a "love match." He claims that Alexander's courteous treatment of Roxane earned him admiration and respect because with out the "sanction of marriage," he "would not approach the only woman who had ever conquered his heart." Women generally didn't have much say in the matter, and we don't really know how Roxane felt about this. But it could have been worse: He could have simply forced a relationship with her without marriage. (Plutarch 303 and 304)
7. Page 83: At the banquet, Cleitus got mad because the entertainers sang a song about Macedonian soldiers who had lost to "barbarians." He felt outraged that a "barbarian" dare make fun of Macedonians. That's when Cleitus turned on Alexander. Before Alexander threw the spear, he threw an apple at Cleitus's head. (Plutarch 308 and 309)
8. Page 85: Callisthenes fancied himself a philosopher, but he was more like a public relations officer. It was his job to tell the Greeks back home how the campaign was going. He also happened to be Aristotle's nephew. Alexander grew so angry with Callisthenes for refusing to bow that he later arrested him on suspicion of treason. (Arrian 223)

CHAPTER 8: Game Over

1. Page 93: According to Rufus, Alexander laid it on thick. He reminded his men about where he had taken them from—and about the riches he had taken them to. Alexander believed that his army could defeat anybody, even if the other Indian armies were bigger and had more elephants than Porus. But he probably lost the men's interest when he claimed, "It is *your* glory, *your* greatness" that he was pursuing. They knew better. By this time, they knew that Alexander was conquering for conquering's sake—and for his own glory. (Rufus 217)

CHAPTER 9: The Beginning of the End

1. Pages 97-98: We can only presume that Alexander's impatience and recklessness were meant to inspire his reluctant men to fight more aggressively. (Arrian 313)
2. Pages 98-99: Alexander's loss would have meant certain death for the stranded army in hostile territory—and his men knew it. (Arrian 318)
3. Page 100: The doctor claimed that even a "slight movement" would have resulted in "grave consequences"—which is why we wanted Alexander held down. (Rufus 224)
4. Page 101: This act of sacrifice captures the essence of Alexander's connection with his men. "It was proof, if anything was, not only of [Alexander's] power of endurance, but also of his genius for leadership." (Arrian 339)
5. Page 102: Alexander claimed that he wanted everybody at the banquet to be his "soldiers by family, not conscription"—in other words, he wanted Greeks and Persians to be one big, happy family—with him in charge, of course. (Rufus 245)
6. Page 103: The men felt that Alexander had done many things to "hurt their feelings, such as adoption of Persian dress," giving Greek armor to Persian officers, and including foreign troops in the Companion cavalry. (Arrian 359)
7. Pages 103-104: It is interesting that this speech—filled with pain and anger at what Alexander considers his men's betrayal—is the longest, most detailed speech Arrian recorded. (Arrian 360-365)
8. Page 104: Harmony was restored when the men kissed Alexander (presumably, the kiss of equals, though the text does not say), picked up their armor, and left, singing a song of victory. (Arrian 366)
9. Page 106: Alexander's last words were dramatic, but unfortunate. By not naming a successor, he paved the way for decades of fighting. (Diodorus 467)
10. Page 106: Calling for equal rights among people of different (albeit conquered) cultures was an amazing breakthrough for the times. (Rufus 245)

CHAPTER 10: Hero—or Monster?

1. Page 114: The holy man's name was Sphines, but the Greeks called him Calanus because he always greeted them with the Indian word, "Cale, which was an Indian saluation." (Plutarch 323)
2. Page 117: We don't know if Alexander's little sister (also named Cleopatra) had any children. It's likely that she did, but no record of her or them exists. Nor do we know what happened to Egypt's Cleopatra's three children, who were shipped back to Rome to be raised by Antony's wife, Octavia. ("Octavia," *Microsoft® Encarta® Online Encyclopedia*, 2005)

BIBLIOGRAPHY

PRIMARY SOURCES (Ancient Biographers)

Arrian, Lucius Favius. *The Campaigns of Alexander*. Translated by Aubrey De Sélincourt. Harmondsworth, Middlesex, England: Penguin Classics, 1958.

Diodurus Siculus. *Library of History: Books XVI–XVII*. Translated by C. Bradford Welles. Cambridge: Harvard University Press, 1963.

Plutarch. *The Age of Alexander*. Translated by Ian Scott-Kilvert. Harmondsworth, Middlesex, England: Penguin Classics, 1973.

Rufus, Quintus Curtius. *The History of Alexander*. Translated by John Yardley, with an introduction and notes by Waldemar Heckel. Harmondsworth, Middlesex, England; New York, New York: Penguin Classics, 1984.

SECONDARY SOURCES ON ALEXANDER

Dodge, Theodore Ayrault. *Alexander*. 1890. Reprint, New York: Da Capo Press, 1996.

Engels, Donald. *Alexander the Great and the Logistics of the Macedonian Army*. Berkeley: University of California Press, 1978.

Fildes, Alan and Fletcher, Joann. *Alexander the Great: Son of the Gods*. Los Angeles: J. Paul Getty Museum, 2002.

Fox, Robin Lane. *Alexander the Great*. London: Penguin Books, 1973.

Green, Peter. *Alexander of Macedon: a Historical Biography*. Berkeley: University of California Press, 1991.

Greenblatt, Miriam. *Alexander the Great and Ancient Greece*. New York: Benchmark Books, 2000.

Krensky, Stephen. *Conqueror and Hero: The Search for Alexander*. Boston: Little, Brown, 1981.

Lamb, Harold. *Alexander of Macedon: The Journey to World's End*. New York: Doubleday & Company, 1946.

Mixer, John. "Alexander's First Great Victory: Significance of the Battle of Granicus for Alexander." *Military History*. December, 1997.

Mossé, Claude. *Alexander, Destiny and Myth*. Translated by Janet Lloyd. Baltimore: The John Hopkins University Press, 2004.

O'Brien, John Maxwell. *Alexander the Great: The Invisible Enemy; A Biography*. London; New York: Routledge, 1992.

Renault, Mary. *The Nature of Alexander*. New York: Pantheon Books, 1975.

Wilcken, Ulrich. *Alexander the Great*. Translated by G.C. Richards, with preface, introduction to Alexander studies, notes, and bibliography by Eugene N. Borza. New York: Norton, 1967.

Wood, Michael. *In the Footsteps of Alexander the Great: A Journey from Greece to Asia*. Berkeley: University of California Press, 1997.

Worthington, Ian. *Alexander the Great: Man and God*. London: Pearson Education Limited, 2004.

SOURCES ON GREEK LIFE AND THE ANCIENT WORLD

"Aristotle." *Concise Routledge Encyclopedia of Philosophy.* London; New York: Routledge, 2000.

Cantor, Norman F. *Antiquity: The Civilization of the Ancient World.* New York: HarperCollins, 2003.

Brann, Eva. *Homeric Moments: Clues to Delight in Reading the* Odyssey *and the* Iliad. Philadelphia: Paul Dry Books, 2002.

Connolly, Peter. *The Greek Armies.* Morristown, NJ: Silver Burdett Co., 1979, 56-72.

Grant, Michael. *From Alexander to Cleopatra: The Hellenistic World.* 1982. Reprint, New York: Charles Scribner's and Sons, 1990.

Homer, *The Iliad.* Translated by W.H.D. Rouse. 1950. Reprint, New York: Signet Classics, 1999.

Honderich, Ted, ed. "Aristotle." *The Oxford Companion to Philosophy.* London: Oxford University Press, 1995.

Kugler, Anthony R. "Playtime." *Dig* 6, no. 4 (April 2004): 8-10.

Neils, Jennifer. "Gym Class." *Dig* 6, no. 4 (April 2004): 20-24.

Oakley, John. "School Days." *Dig* 6, no. 4 (April 2004): 12-14.

Parker, Steve. *Aristotle and Scientific Thought.* 1994. Reprint, New York: Chelsea House, 1995.

Quennell, Marjorie and C.H.B. *Everyday Things in Ancient Greece.* New York: GP Putnam's Sons, 1954.

Rees, Rosemary. *The Ancient Greeks.* Crystal Lake, Illinois: Heinemann, 1997.

Rouse, W.H.D. *Gods, Heroes and Men of Ancient Greece.* 1934. Reprint, Cambridge: Signet Classics, 1957.

Schomp, Virginia. *The Ancient Greeks.* Tarrytown, New York: Benchmark Books, 1996.

Warry, John. *Warfare in the Classical World: An Illustrated Encyclopedia of Weapon, Warriors, and Warfare in the Ancient Civilizations of Greece and Rome.* 1980. Reprint, Norman: University of Oklahoma Press, 2002.

What Life Was Like at the Dawn of Democracy. New York: Time-Life Books, 1997.

Woff, Richard. *The Ancient Greek Olympics.* New York: Oxford University Press, 1999.

WEB SOURCES

www.pothos.org A serious Web site for Alexander the Great scholars and lay Alex fans. Scholarly articles, excellent discussion forum, and a guide to the best books on Alexander.

www.alexanderthegreat.gr/index.html Great resource for overview articles on Alexander, as well as links to other Alexander sites.

www.livius.org/greece.html Comprehensive site for articles about key people and events in the ancient world.

www.isidore-of-seville.com/Alexanderama.html Features more than 1,000 resources on Alexander, plus 400 images (in sculpture and paintings) of Alexander from the ancient world to medieval times.

INDEX